TOTALLY SICK & OFFENSIVE JOKES FOR THE LOCKDOWN 2020

J. J. Wilkinson

All profits from this book will be used to help care workers who have put themselves on the "front line" to keep the elderly safe

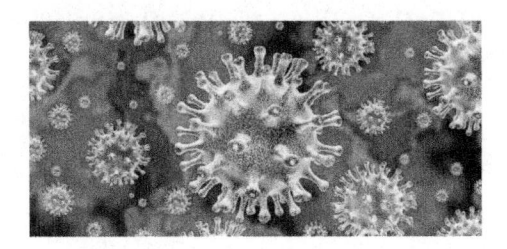

I know a great joke about Corona Virus, you probably won't get it though.

Does anyone know if your allowed to have a shower yet, or do we just keep washing our hands.

If I get quarantined for two weeks with my wife and I die. I can assure you it was not the virus that killed me.

With all this talk of Corona Virus, the people who make sanitising gel are rubbing their hands together.

I went to the chemist today and asked the assistant "what kills the Corona Virus?" She replied to me "Ammonia Cleaner" I said "Oh, I am sorry, I thought you worked here"

Day 3 without sports. Found a lady sitting on my couch yesterday. Apparently she is my wife. She seems nice.

Since everybody has now started washing their hands, the peanuts at the bar have lost their taste.

They said that a mask and gloves were enough to go to the supermarket. They lied, everyone else has clothes on.

Before Corona Virus I used to cough to cover a fart, now I fart to cover a cough.

Definition of Irony - When the Year Of The Rat starts with a plague.

My body has absorbed so much soap and disinfectant lately, now when I pee I clean the toilet.

Back in the day the only time we started panic buying was when the bartender yelled "last call"

I think it is great that people are finally starting to drink water, wipe their ass and wash their hands.

Ok, so if the Corona Virus isn't about beer, why do I keep hearing about cases of it?

To the people who bought 20 bottles of soap leaving none of the shelves for others, you do realise that to stop getting Coronavirus, you need other people washing their hands too.

Chuck Norris has been exposed to the Coronavirus. The virus is now in quarantine for a month.

Chinese doctors have confirmed the name of the first person to contract Coronavirus. His name is Ah-Chu.

Don't worry, the Corona Virus won't last long... It was made in China.

To those who are complaining about the quarantine period and curfews, just remember that your grandparents were called to war, you are being called to sit on the couch and watch Netflix. You can do this.

How come the liquor stores don't have empty shelves? Don't people understand that they will be quarantined with their spouses and kids?

Mexico is asking Trump to hurry up and build the wall NOW!

During self isolation..
Dogs: "Oh My god, you're here all day and this is the best as I can love you, see you, be with you and follow you! I am so excited be-

cause you are the greatest and I love you being here so much!
Cats: "What the hell are you still doing here?"

I don't know why my fishing buddy is worried about Coronavirus, he never catches anything.

Social distancing rule: If you can smell their fart, move further apart.

The Coronavirus has achieved what no female has every been able to achieve. It has cancelled sports, closed all bars and kept all guys at home!

I don't know why the weatherman is still bothering. Its going to be 21 degrees with fluorescent lighting all week!

Day 6 quarantine: preparing to take out the garbage… so excited.. can't decide what to wear.

There is a gap in your CV, what were you doing in 2020? I was washing my hands!

A man came to the train station. Where are you going asked the policeman on guard. To jeopardy answers the man. No such place says the police. Oh, yes there is says the man, it said in the news, due to the coronavirus thousands of jobs in jeopardy…

"Darling…fancy putting on a nurses uniform"? "Ooh, cheeky boy…you feeling horny"? "Nah…we've run out of bread"!

Anyone wishing to show their appreciation for Amazon delivery drivers are asked to clap at their homes tomorrow anytime between 9am and 6pm.

A man doesn't walk into a pub……….

2019: "work hard at school or you'll end up packing shelves for a living"….. 2020: "most secure job in the country, packing shelves"

As Italy struggles to cremate the dead, Angel Merkel has assured assured German citizens that Germany can cremate up to six million.

As if it wasn't bad enough being Dyslexic, now I've got the Racoon virus.

Don't go to the pub. Don't meet up with your friends. Don't come home with an infection. Honestly, Boris Johnson is starting to sound like my fucking girlfriend.

ISIS: We are reluctantly laying off all suicide bombers , due to insufficient crowd sizes.

China have got what they have always wanted. To CORONISE the world!!!

My cat just asked me if I want the radio leaving on while he goes out.

Staff at St Thomas' have reported Boris Johnson is looking bloated, sweaty, generally disheveled and talking incoherently. A Spokesperson said.. "It's encouraging to see him look like his old self again."

The amount of jokes about coronavirus virus has reached worrying numbers. Scientists claim we are in the middle of a pundemic

Single woman with hand sanitizer would like to meet a single man with toilet rolls for good clean fun.

When shopping in Harrods, ensure people stay at least two meters away from you by holding a Lidl carrier bag.

Apparently, gluten allergies don't exist during food shortages.

I like my girls how I like my Covid. 19 and easily spread.

Let's take a moment to think of Philip Schofield. The poor bugger only just came out and now he's being told he's got to stay in.

This corona virus must be serious. My local Burger King have cleaned their tables twice today.

ME: Dial 999. Police, please
POLICE: Police
ME: Hi. Two hooded men are robbing my shed.
POLICE: Sorry, we have no resources. There's nothing we can do.
ME: They are standing less than 1 metre apart.
POLICE: Keep them there - we'll be there in 5.

So how come it's only men & women getting killed by this Coronavirus? How come all the other 800 genders aren't getting wiped out?

5 sleeps till putting the bins out

Corona virus has turned us all into dogs. We roam around the house looking for food. We're told "No!" If we get too close to strangers. And the thought of a car ride sends us wild with excitement.

Of course Trump has banned all travel from Europe. He thinks germs come from Germany.

Whoever said one person can't change the world never ate an undercooked bat

I couldn't get any bread in the supermarket today so I went to the park and threw I.O.U's to the ducks.

A friend in Germany tells me everyone's panic buying sausages and cheese. It's the Wurst Käse scenario.

I can remember the days when we used to smoke in pubs, now we can't even drink in them.

Prince William: "Hi Harry. Dad has COVID-19." Prince Harry: "Yours might have."

In light of recent of panic buying UK supermarkets have introduced purchase limits.
Asda: 2 hand sanitisers, 24 toilet rolls max.
Tesco: 1 Hand sanitiser, 18 toilet rolls & 2kg rice.

Co-op: 12 rolls toilet paper, 1 Kg rice.
Aldi: 2 Trumpets, 1 diving suit & a MIG welder.

Breaking news, person dies from something other than the Coronavirus.

Down South they're stockpiling toilet rolls and hoarding pasta. Up North we're licking door handles to try and get two weeks off work.

The kid I hired to clean up poop in my yard just realized I don't have a dog

I bet the Fritzl kids would give anything to be back in that basement now!

I ordered a chinese takeaway, a chinese driver comes to the door and I walked out to meet him. He then started shouting "isolate isolate". I said "Mate your'e not that late, I only ordered 10 minutes ago".

At last... Something positive from the Prime Minister.

I'm not saying the people panic buying rice and pasta are misguided, but it hasn't worked for China or Italy.......

I've just spent a few weeks in isolation, locked in my bedroom, masturbating to porn hub and reading sick jokes... I was going to venture out to the shops today, until I turned on the news and heard about this corona virus thingy.

Experts are confident that washing our hands regularly will combat coronavirus but say they are expecting an outbreak of OCD.

Virus or not, me and my partner are just having a couple of hours down Skegness seafront. We've toured the arcades, had a couple of rides and got some ace photos eating candy floss in 'kiss me quick' hats.
My boss even rang up to see how we're getting on .. I told him, "All quiet here Sarg, we've not had to make any arrests."

Show your wealth off by throwing a toilet roll on the pitch at a crap football match.
Symptoms are mild and he is said to be "sponging from home"

I was devastated to hear about Robbie Williams during the current outbreak. Apparently he's fine.

Breaking news:
USA Corona virus death toll rises to 11. Student with gun: "Hold my beer..."

The wife and I have been in lockdown for eight days now. One thing's for sure, there's no way I'm retiring.

just got back from Vietnam, and I've tested positive for COViD nnnnn19

During this virus lockdown I'm bored, so I decided to hold a wet t-shirt contest. Looking at them hanging on the line, I've decided I like my red one the best.

As many schools across the United States close down due to coronavirus, it is hoped lives will be saved due to less school shootings.

Thunderbirds 2020. Go and fetch the Rolls, Parker. Do you want the Andrex or Tesco home brand, Milady?.

I was in a supermarket in Glasgow today and the food shortage situation has gotten so bad, people were actually buying fruit and veg

Things are getting really desperate in my house because of the Coronavirus. Today I've had to break open the Lynx Africa gift set I got for Christmas.

Does anybody know how long you have to wait before you can safely eat a family member who has died from Coronavirus. Asking for a friend.

Studies have confirmed that women can significantly increase their immunity to COVID 19 by ingesting semen!..[worth a try anyway?]

Good to see all the women are socially distancing their car tyres at least 2 meters from the white lines in the supermarket car park today.

I can't find any bog roll in my local shops so I've started panic buying imodium

Britain is currently third in the world table of Coronavirus deaths. Come on you lot, a bit more effort and we can win this thing.

At this current time, apparently dressing up completely as the Grim Reaper and going and standing in close proximity to older people at the supermarket is considered "Massively insensitive."

My wife Ivy has been in isolation for over a week now. She's climbing the walls.

Breaking News:
DFS sale has officially ended

Anyone know how Fred West got away with killing his family for so long? Asking for a friend

In the spirit of equality, the Government has announced that, from tomorrow, the homeless are allowed one 30 minute session of indoor exercise per day.

I can't wait to get out of isolation and back to work. So I can book a week off.

I've just seen on the news that they are talking about rationing books. Who the fuck is panic buying books

Prince Charles has had his latest test results back. He's still not Harry's dad.

London's ExCel Centre is about to be filled with 4000 coronavirus patients. Who would want to go and look at those?

My Mother-In-Law was playing holy fuck about not being able to buy a toilet roll for love nor money, I could see she was upset about this so I thought I'd cheer her up.
I took her out for a red hot Vindaloo and six pints of Guinness.

Oh how I wish it was January again and all we had to worry about was nuclear war.

Radio One and stations all over Europe this morning played 'You'll Never Walk alone' at the same time. I'm pretty sure Europe's 'The Final Countdown' would have been a better choice.

Breaking News: Russian footballer Ivor Chestikov has tested possible for Covid-19

There once was an NHS boffin
Who woke up to find himself coughing
A virus he'd caught
Now his family have bought
A coffin to carry him off in

Boris Johnson will give his daily coronavirus update speech from his hospital bed after breakfast. Today's will consist of a large helping of waffle.

What if this Coronavirus is just Man Flu and now women are realising just how bad we've had it for years?

My grandmother currently has a very high temperature and can't breathe. It's got nothing to do with the corona virus...she is in the middle of being cremated.

As Rick Astley once said....

Were no strangers to gloves,
You know the rules and so do I,
Corona Lockdowns what I'm thinking of,
You don't want this cough its very very dry,

J. J. WILKINSON

I just wanna tell you how I'm sneezing,
Gotta make you understand.

Never gonna hit the pub,
Never gonna go downtown,
Never gonna run around,
And contract Flu.
Never gonna make you die,
Never gonna go Shanghai,
Never gonna try a bat,
And infect you.

We've been In Quarantine for oh so long,
Your body's aching but you're too scared to say it,
Inside we both know what's been going on,
We know the virus and we're gonna slay it,
And if you ask me how I'm feeling,
Don't tell me you're too Ill to see.

Never gonna hit the pub,
Never gonna go downtown,
Never gonna run around,
And contract Flu.
Never gonna make you die,
Never gonna go Shanghai,
Never gonna try a bat,
And infect you.

They've run out of sausages in Germany so they're having to make new ones out of seabirds. It's a tern for the wurst.

Due to the current financial situation caused by the Coronna virus and the slowdown of the economy, the Government has decided to implement the following schemes to help improve future employment and therefore stimulate the economy.
Workers of 50 years of age or more will be forced into retirement. This scheme will be known as RAPE. (Retire aged persons early).
Those selected to be RAPED can apply for the SHAFT benefits.

(Special help after forced termination)
Those chosen to be RAPED or SHAFTED will be reviewed under the SCREW programme. (System covering retired early workers). A person can only be RAPED once, SHAFTED twice, but can be SCREWED as many times as the Government sees fit.
Those that get RAPED can get AIDS (Additional income for dependants & spouses) or HERPES (Half earnings for retired early severence)

Food shortages in the supermarkets....hot tip.....Whiskas Beef cat food makes an excellent chilli con carne, not only does it taste great but with balanced mineral levels it supports a healthy urinary tract, the zinc content ensures a healthy skin and there are no added artificial flavours, colours or preservatives.
The only down side is the constant pestering by the cat as you make it.

I'm really looking forward to Michael Palins new series "around the house in 80 days "

Top tip, if your down to your last sheet of Andrex and you have the flu, BLOW YOUR NOSE FIRST!

Never in human history has constipation been counted as a blessing before.

Flights grounded. Factories closed. Hardly any traffic on the roads. I think Greta is behind this.

Money wise, I am set for life. Just as long as I contract coronavirus and die next Tuesday.

Phoned 111 today because of shortness of breath and chest pain. Doctor said not to worry I don't have coronavirus, it's only a heart attack

Yesterday, the French authorities deployed the military to supermarkets, in order to keep them secure and ensure social distancing is being respected.

However, after one old lady coughed, the armed forces have capitulated and are now negotiating terms of surrender with the shoppers.

Everyone is impressed with Dyson for designing a new ventilator so fast. Little do they know its just a vac with the wires swapped over.

Doesn't Balmoral count as a second holiday home then? Very strange indeed.

Oh dear, no school dinners and McDonald's closing, all we need now is for the Pot Noodle factory to close and we'll have more starving kids than Africa.

PUBLIC SERVICE ANNOUNCEMENT:
Corona Virus origin traced - IT WAS CREATED BY WOMEN

Think about it, lads...

1 - Sport postponed for months
2 - Advised against going to the pub
3 - Don't leave the house for a fortnight (so you can finally get those odd jobs done)
4 - Symptoms are flu-like (THEY KNOW THAT'S OUR KRYPTONITE)
5 - They even had the audacity to name it after a beer!

Good news for heavy gamblers...Only a couple of weeks til' the Two Flies Walking Up A Wall season begins.

According to researchers, a new study on mice offers hope for a vaccine against coronavirus Which is all very well, if you happen to be a fucking mouse.

With the ban on large gatherings of people, only the Lib Dems will be having a conference this year.

If coronavirus and food shortages get any worse, I'm thinking of rowing a rubber dinghy to Africa for a better life.

What a shame to see so many of the French surrendering to the virus.

Sorry folks Monday was the 90 day satisfaction guarantee deadline to get your money back on 2020.

There are always alternatives if you cant go out. I'm unable to go to the Gym, So instead i google 'Women in Yoga pants' on my laptop.

I wonder what the vegans do when they realise that the vaccine for Coronavirus is currently being tested on animals?

The richest 10% own 50% of all the wealth.
The dumbest 10% own 50% of all the toilet paper.

I'm thinking of booking myself into a hotel for a few days. Just to get the free soap and bog roll!

We all know someone who'll get Covid-20.
If you've had one shit, they've had two.
If you have a black cat, they have a blacker cat.
If you've been to Tenerife, they've been to Elevenarife.

Cellmate: "I have Coronavirus"
Weinstein: #metoo

My mother in law, who is in her late eighties, only lives just around the corner from me.
She's been told not to leave the house until this pandemic is over. However i'm confident she wont get the coronavirus.
She'll starve to death before then.

Corona-nation Street starts on ITV tonight. It's a soap, so should be effective against germs

Are the BBC rubbing it in by showing Ready Steady Cook? Like we can buy ingredients to cook meals these days...

it's only Quarantine if it's in the Quarante region of France. Other than that it's just sparkling isolation

The NHS has urgently requested that all top flight football physiotherapists help out. Their ability to cure what seem to be critical injuries in less than 30 seconds will soon put an end to this disaster.

These are strange times because I'm spending money on things I never normally would. Like the wife & kids.

> if you OR your partner is ginger, there's a 50% chance your children will be.
>
> THINK.

My wife is really mad at the fact that I have no sense of direction.

So I packed up my stuff and right.

Today, my son asked "Can I have a book mark?" and I burst into tears. 11 years old and he still doesn't know my name is Brian.

DAD: I was just listening to the radio on my way into town, apparently an actress just killed herself.
MOM: Oh my! Who!?
DAD: Uh, I can't remember... I think her name was Reese something?
MOM: WITHERSPOON!!!!!???????
DAD: No, it was with a knife...

How do you make holy water? You boil the hell out of it.

I bought some shoes from a drug dealer. I don't know what he laced them with, but I was tripping all day!

Did you know the first French fries weren't actually cooked in France? They were cooked in Greece.

If a child refuses to sleep during nap time, are they guilty of resisting a rest?

The secret service isn't allowed to yell "Get down!" anymore when the president is about to be attacked. Now they have to yell "Donald, duck!"

What do you call someone with no body and no nose? Nobody knows.

I ordered a chicken and an egg from Amazon. I'll let you know

What is the least spoken language in the world? Sign language

My daughter screeched, "Daaaaaad, you haven't listened to one word I've said, have you!?" What a strange way to start a conversation with me...

A slice of apple pie is $2.50 in Jamaica and $3.00 in the Bahamas. These are the pie rates of the Caribbean.

My friend keeps saying "cheer up man it could be worse, you could be stuck underground in a hole full of water." I know he means well.

Why can't you hear a pterodactyl go to the bathroom? Because the pee is silent.

Spring is here! I got so excited I wet my plants!

3 unwritten rules of life...
1.
2.
3.

If you see a robbery at an Apple Store does that make you an iWitness?

Why did the invisible man turn down the job offer? He couldn't see himself doing it.

What's the best part about living in Switzerland? I don't know, but the flag is a big plus.

Why couldn't the bike standup by itself? It was two tired.

What do you call a deer with no eyes? No idea!

Two guys walk into a bar, the third one ducks.

How many tickles does it take to make an octopus laugh? Ten-tickles.

To call the whole Elon Musk controversy "Elon-Gate" seems like a bit of a stretch.

What noise does a 747 make when it bounces? Boeing, Boeing, Boeing.

Did you hear about the circus fire? It was in tents!

I'm only familiar with 25 letters in the English language. I don't know why.

As a lumberjack, I know that I've cut exactly 2,417 trees. I know because every time I cut one, I keep a log.

I was interrogated over the theft of a cheese toastie. Man, they really grilled me.

You heard of that new band 1023MB? They're good but they haven't got a gig yet.

What do you call a lonely cheese? Provolone.

I told my 14 year old son I thought 'Fortnite' was a stupid name for a computer game. I think it is just too weak.

How do you make a Kleenex dance? Put a little boogie in it!

I think my wife is putting glue on my antique weapons collection. She denies it but I'm sticking to my guns!

I got a hen to regularly count her own eggs. She's a real mathama-chicken!

Why do trees seem suspicious on sunny days? They just seem a little shady!

What did the policeman say to his belly button? You're under a vest!

Last night I had a dream that I weighed less than a thousandth of a gram. I was like, 0mg.

A cheese factory exploded in France. Da brie is everywhere!

I've been bored recently so I've decided to take up fencing. The neighbors said they will call the police unless I put it back.

Why did the math book look so sad? Because of all of its problems!

I don't really like funerals that start before noon. I guess I'm just not a mourning person!

If two vegans get in a fight, is it still considered a beef?

One of my favorite memories as a kid was when my brothers used to put me inside a tire and roll me down a hill. They were Goodyears!

Did you hear about the Italian chef who died? He pasta way!

What's orange and sounds like a parrot? A carrot!

I invented a new word today: Plagiarism!

What do you call a donkey with only three legs? A wonkey!

After dinner, my wife asked if I could clear the table. I needed a running start, but I made it!

Why is Peter Pan always flying? He neverlands!

What's a ninja's favorite type of shoes? Sneakers!

I know a lot of jokes about retired people but none of them work!

What do Santa's elves listen to ask they work? Wrap music!

I like telling Dad jokes. Sometimes he laughs!

To whoever stole my copy of Microsoft Office, I will find you. You have my Word!

I used to work in a shoe-recycling shop. It was sole destroying!

My boss told me to have a good day. So I went home!

I'm so good at sleeping I can do it with my eyes closed!

This graveyard looks overcrowded. People must be dying to get in there!

My friend says to me, "What rhymes with orange?" And I told him, "No it doesn't!"

My wife told me I had to stop acting like a flamingo. So I had to put my foot down!

I told my girlfriend she drew her eyebrows too high. She seemed surprised!

Did I tell you the time I fell in love during a backflip? I was heels over head!

My uncle named his dogs Rolex and Timex. They're his watch dogs!

I would avoid the sushi if I was you. It's a little fishy!

Five out of four people admit they're bad with fractions!

Two goldfish are in a tank. One says to the other, "Do you know how to drive this thing?"

What do sprinters eat before a race? Nothing, they fast!

What concert costs just 45 cents? 50 Cent featuring Nickelback!

Why did the scarecrow win an award? Because he was outstanding in his field!

What do you call a mac 'n' cheese that gets all up in your face? Too close for comfort food!

Why do melons have weddings? Because they cantaloupe!

What's the difference between a poorly dressed man on a tricycle and a well-dressed man on a bicycle? Attire!

How many apples grow on a tree? All of them!

Did you hear the rumor about butter? Well, I'm not going to spread it!

Did you hear about the guy who invented Lifesavers? They say he made a mint!

Why do you never see elephants hiding in trees? Because they're so good at it!

How does a penguin build its house? Igloos it together!

Why did the old man fall in the well? Because he couldn't see that well!

Why don't skeletons ever go trick or treating? Because they have no body to go with!

What did the drummer call his twin daughters? Anna one, Anna two!

How did Darth Vader know what Luke got him for Christmas? He felt his presents!

Did you hear about the chameleon who couldn't change color? He had a reptile dysfunction.

I wanted to go on a diet, but I feel like I have way too much on my plate right now.
Want to hear a joke about construction? I'm still working on it.

What sound does a witches car make? Broom Broom

To whoever stole my copy of Microsoft Office, I will find you. You have my Word!

What's that Nevada city where all the dentists visit? Floss Vegas.

Atheism is a non-prophet organization.

Why did the picture go to jail? Because it was framed.

What do you call a bear without any teeth? A gummy bear!

The shovel was a ground-breaking invention.

Does anyone need an ark? I Noah guy!

To the man in the wheelchair that stole my camouflage jacket... You can hide but you can't run.

The rotation of earth really makes my day.

What's black and white and goes around and around? A penguin in a revolving door.

Why do you never see elephants hiding in trees? Because they're so good at it.

Did you hear about the kidnapping at school? It's fine, he woke up.

What did the caretaker say when they jumped out of the store cupboard? "Supplies!"

If a child refuses to sleep during nap time, are they guilty of resisting a rest?

A furniture store keeps calling me. All I wanted was one night stand.

I used to work in a shoe recycling shop. It was sole destroying.

What do you call a man who can't stand? Neil.

I'm thinking about removing my spine. I feel like it's only holding me back.

Why are cats bad storytellers? Because they only have one tale.

Why was the belt sent to jail? For holding up a pair of pants!

What do you call a baby monkey? A chimp off the old block.

What's an astronaut's favorite part of a computer? The space bar.

Do you think glass coffins will be a success? Remains to be seen.

What lies at the bottom of the ocean and twitches? A nervous wreck.

What happens when a frogs car dies? He needs a jump. If that doesn't work he has to get it toad.

Which bear is the most condescending? A pan-duh!

Why are elevator jokes so classic and good? They work on many levels.

What do you call a pudgy psychic? A four-chin teller.

My wife asked me to stop singing "Wonderwall" to her. I said maybe –

What do you call a naughty lamb dressed up like a skeleton for Halloween? Baaad to the bone.

Want to know why nurses like red crayons? Sometimes they have to draw blood.

What would the Terminator be called in his retirement? The Ex-terminator.

My wife asked me to go get 6 cans of Sprite from the grocery store. I realized when I got home that I had picked 7 up.

Why do bees have sticky hair? Because they use a honeycomb.

Why do some couples go to the gym? Because they want their relationship to work out.

What's the most detail-oriented ocean? The Pacific.

How can you tell it's a dogwood tree? By the bark.

Which state has the most streets? Rhode Island.

What do you call 26 letters that went for a swim? Alphawetical.

What's the name of a very polite, European body of water? Mersey.

Why was the color green notoriously single? It was always so jaded.

I used to hate facial hair, but then it grew on me.

I want to make a brief joke, but it's a little cheesy.

Why did the coach go to the bank? To get his quarterback.

How do celebrities stay cool? They have many fans.

Sundays are always a little sad, but the day before is a sadder day.

I've been thinking about taking up meditation. I figure it's better than sitting around doing nothing.

Dogs can't operate MRI machines. But cat scan.

What did the flowers do when the bride walked down the aisle? They rose.

It takes guts to be an organ donor.

What does "Rockin' Robin" do when she's bored? Tweet.

I lost my job at the bank on my first day. A woman asked me to check her balance, so I pushed her over.

How do you row a canoe filled with puppies? Bring out the doggy paddle.

Singing in the shower is fun until you get soap in your mouth. Then it becomes a soap opera.

Why were the utensils stuck together? They were spooning.

What's a crafty dancer's favorite hobby? Cutting a rug.

What kind of shoes does a lazy person wear? Loafers.

Why is cold water so insecure? Because it's never called hot.

I was going to tell a time-traveling joke, but you guys didn't like it.

I told my doctor I heard buzzing, but he said it's just a bug going around.

What did the accountant say while auditing a document? This is taxing.

What did the two pieces of bread say on their wedding day? It was loaf at first sight.

If the early bird gets the worm, I'll sleep in until there's pancakes.

Someone told me that I should write a book. I said, "That's a novel concept."

Why do dads feel the need to tell such bad jokes? They just want to help you become a groan up.

Why are spiders so smart? They can find everything on the web.

RIP boiled water—you will be mist.

What do you call two octopuses that look the same? Itenticle.

What has one head, one foot, and four legs? A bed.

Sore throats are a pain in the neck.

What does a house wear? Address.

What's red and smells like blue paint? Red paint.

What do you call an unpredictable camera? A loose Canon.

I'm so good at sleeping, I can do it with my eyes closed.

People are usually shocked that I have a Police record. But I love their greatest hits!

What do you call a fibbing cat? A lion.

Why shouldn't you write with a broken pencil? Because it's pointless.

How do you weigh a millennial? In Instagrams.

Did you hear about the cartoonist found dead at his home? Details are sketchy.

Last night my wife and I watched two DVDs back to back. Luckily I was the one facing the TV.

Where did Napoleon keep his armies? Up his sleevies!

Did you hear about the guy who had his left side cut off? He's all right now!

I slept like a log last night. Woke up in the fireplace!

I went to a seafood disco last week! Pulled a mussel!

I fear for the calendar. It's days are numbered.

Did you hear about the hungry clock. It went back four seconds.

I heard there is a new shop called Moderation. They have everything in there.

An invisible man married and invisable women. The kids were nothing to look at.

I gave away all my used batteries today. Free of charge!

I remember the first time I saw a universal remote control. I thought to myself 'well this changes everything'.

I stayed up all night wondering where the sun went. Then it dawned on me.

What is the difference between an angry circus owner and a Roman barber? One is a raving showman, the other is a shaving roman.

Have you ever tried to eat a clock? It's very time consuming.

England doesn't have a kidney bank. But it does have a Liverpool.

Yesterday I accidentally swallowed some food colouring. The doctor says i'm ok, but i feel like i've dyed a little inside.

I don't trust stairs because they're always up to something.

I wasn't going to get a brain transplant. But then I changed my mind.

Two hats were hanging on a hat rack. One said 'You stay here, i'll go on a head'.

Did you hear about the girl who quit her job at the doughnut factory? She was fed up with the hole business.

People are making apocalypse jokes like there is no tomorrow!

Did you hear the story about the haunted lift? It really raised my spirits!

I dreamt about drowning in an ocean made of orange pop last night. It took me a while to work out it was just a Fanta Sea.

I'd tell you a chemistry joke but I know i wouldn't get a reaction.

What did the late tomato say to the other tomatoes? Don't worry i'll ketchup.

Can I watch TV? Yes but don't turn it on.

What did the fish say when it swam into a wall? Damn!

Have you heard of a music group called Cellophane? They mainly wrap.

A red and blue ship have collided in the Carribean sea. Apparently the suvivors are marooned.

A policy officer caught two kids playing with a firework and a car battery. He charged one and let the other off.

What do you call a group of killer whales playing instruments? An Orca-stra!

Why was the big cat disqualified from the race? Because it was a cheetah!

What is the worst combination of two sicknesses? Diarrhea and Alzheimer. You're running, but you don't know where.

Which Spice Girl can carry the most petrol? Geri can.

How do you light up a football stadium? With a football match.

What do you call it when a hen looks at a lettuce? A chicken caesar salad.

What do you call a Mexican whose vehicle has been stolen? Carlos.

I met some obsessive chess players in a hotel reception, going on about how good they were. They were chess-nuts boasting in an open foyer.

A dad is washing his car with his son. The son says: "Dad, can't you use a sponge?"

I accidentally handed my wife the superglue instead of her lipstick. She still isn't talking to me.

Two cats swam the English Channel. They were called One Two Three and Un Deux Trois. Which cat won? One Two Three, because Un Deux Trois cat sank.

Dad: Can I administer my own anaesthetic? Surgeon: Go ahead - knock yourself out.

I refused to believe that my dad was stealing from his job as a road worker. But when I went round to his house all the signs were there.

Two sailors see an enormous hand come out of the sea. It moves all the way over to one side, then all the way over to the other. One sailor says to the other: "Wow, did you see the size of that wave?"

A Dutchman has invented shoes that record how many miles you've walked. Clever clogs.

Two parrots are sitting on a perch. One says to the other: "Can you smell fish?"

Lots of cars in a multi- storey car park have been broken into.

That's wrong on so many levels.

What's a foot long and slippery? A slipper.

A neutron walks into a pub and orders a pint. The barman says he won't take its money: "No charge."

Why don't ants get ill? Because they have antibodies.

What should you call a woman whose voice sounds like an ambulance? Nina.

How do you organise a party in space? Plan it.

Two TV aerials got married. The ceremony was boring, but the reception was great.

Why did the pony ask for a glass of water? Because he was a little horse.

Why did the Mexican man push his wife off a cliff? Tequila.

What did the buffalo say to his son when he dropped him off at school? "Bison."

What do you call a cow with a twitch? Beef jerky.

I once bought a dog from a blacksmith. As soon as I got it home, it made a bolt for the door.

I tripped over my wifes bra, It appeared to be a booby trap

For my birthday my children gave me an alarm clock that sweared at me instead of buzzing. It was quite a rude awakening

A man was recently hospitalised with 6 plastic horses inside of him. The doctor is describing his condition as stable.

I can always tell if someone is lying just by looking at them, I can also tell if they are standing.

It's a 5 minute walk from my house to the pub. It's a 35 minute walk from the pub to my house. The difference is staggering.

A locksmith had to go to court to give evidence last week. Apparently he was the key witness.

Today I actually saw a dwarf prisoner climbing down a wall I thought to myself, "now that's a little condescending"

How do you find Will Smith in a snowstorm? Look for the fresh prints.

How many apples grow on a tree? All of them.

Chris Hemsworth is Australian and Thor is from space does that make him an Australien

I read that by law you must turn on your headlights when it's raining in Sweden but how am I supposed to know when it is raining in Sweden?

Two wind turbines stand in a field. One says to the other, "So, what kind of music are you into?" The other replies, "I'm a huge metal fan."

What did the grape do when he got stepped on? He let out a little wine.

Me: There are millions of camels out here in the desert. Daughter: I can't see any! Me: That's because they're camelflaged

I don't play soccer because I enjoy the sport. I'm just doing it for kicks.

People don't like having to bend over to get their drinks. We really need to raise the bar.

Cop: I am arresting you for illegally downloading the entire wikipedia Me: Wait! I can explain everything!

I bought a wooden car last week. Wooden engine, wooden doors, wooden wheels, wooden seats, put the wooden key in the wooden ignition.. Wooden start

A man goes to a funeral and asks the widow "Mind if I say a word?". The widow replies "Please do". The man clears his throat and says "Bargain". The widow replies "Thanks, that means a great deal".

Shout out to the people asking what the opposite of in is.

Did you hear about the guy who invented the door knocker? He won the no-bell prize.

My boss is threatening to fire the employee with the worst posture. I have a hunch, it may be me.

I was a doctor for a while but then I quit, I didn't have enough patience.

All flights at the John Lennon Airport are grounded. Just imagine all the people.

What two things can you never eat for breakfast? Lunch and Dinner.

What tastes better than it smells? A Tongue.

What kind of room has no doors or windows? A Mushroom.

During what month do people sleep the least? February, it's the shortest month.

What goes up and never comes down? Your Age.

What word becomes shorter when you add two letters to it? Short

Before Mt. Everest was discovered, what was the highest mountain in the world? Mt. Everest; it just wasn't discovered yet.

How much dirt is there in a hole that measures two feet by three feet by four feet? There is no dirt because it is a hole.

What has four wheels and flies? A garbage truck.

What gets wetter the more it dries? A towel.

Which word in the dictionary is spelled incorrectly? Incorrectly

You can't keep this until you have given it. A promise.

What grows when it eats, but dies when it drinks? Fire.

What spends all the time on the floor but never gets dirty? Your Shadow.

How many months in the year have 28 days? All of them.

A man goes out in heavy rain with nothing to protect him from it. His hair doesn't get wet. How does he do that? He is bald.

What part of the chicken has the most feathers? The Outside.

What goes up and down but never moves? The stairs.

Ten ladies tried to fit under a small umbrella, none of them got wet. How did they do it? It wasn't raining!

What sounds like a sneeze and is made out of leather? A shoe

What always goes to sleep with shoes on? A horse

Imagine The Titanic with a lisp.
It's unthinkable.

I phoned the Child Abuse Hotline.

A kid answered, called me a cunt and told me to fuck off.

Breaking news...........
Two Muslims have crashed a speedboat into the Thames barrier in London.
Police think it might be the start of Ram-a-dam.

You gotta hand it to midgets.
Because some times they can't reach.

Have you noticed how many F1 drivers have names linked to Scottish towns?
Stirling Moss, Lewis Hamilton, Eddie Irvine.......Ayr Town Centre....

Breaking news, midget holds seance for charity and runs off with the takings.
Small medium at large.

I was in the kitchen when a flying insect came through the window and exploded.
I think it was a jihaddy longlegs.

Talk about coincidence - BBC NEWS: Three Cliff Walkers have fallen to their death on an expedition....
Can't believe they all had the same name....

I just applied for a job in the Citroen factory.
I had to send in 2CVs.

I ordered a thesaurus from Amazon but when it was delivered all the pages were blank.
I have no words to describe how angry I am.

We were so poor growing up that for breakfast we had ordinary K

To the Scumbag that stole 300 cans of RedBull from my shop,
I don't know how you can sleep at night.

I couldn't believe it today when my son came home with two armchairs and a settee.

I've told him a million times, never accept suites from strangers.

My mate broke his leg so I went to see him at home.
"How are you mate?"
"Yeah I'm okay. But do me a favour mate. Go fetch my slippers from upstairs. My feet are freezing."
I went upstairs and found his two gorgeous 19 year old daughters lying naked on the bed.
I said "Your dad's sent me up here to have sex with both of you."
They respond "Get away with ya... Prove it."
I shouted downstairs "Hey, mate! Both of them?"
He shouted back "Of course both of them! What's the point in fucking one?"

I couldn't undo the buttons on my jumper, so i tried pulling it over my head but got it stuck.
I'm in A&E now waiting to see a cardyologist.

The only thing flat-earthers fear ……. is sphere itself.

I love taking pictures of myself standing next to boiling water..
Doctor says I've got selfie steam issues..

"Diana!" I said greeting my Mother-In-Law as she walked through the door...
She said, "My name's Anna."
I said, "Yeah, I know."

There's a nudist convention in my town tomorrow.
I might go if I've got nothing on.

I'm Having trouble finding out what 51, 6 and 500 are in Roman numerals!!!
I'm LIVID

A bloke starts his new job at the zoo and is given three tasks.
First is to clear the exotic fish pool of weeds. As he does so, a huge fish jumps out of the water and bites him. To show the fish who's boss, he beats it to death with a spade.

Realising his employer won't be best pleased, he disposes of the fish by feeding it to the Lions.
Moving on to the second job of clearing out the Chimp house, he gets attacked by the chimps who pelt him with coconuts. He swipes at two of the chimps with his spade, killing them both. 'Feed them to the lions.' He says to himself. So he hurls the corpses into the Lion enclosure.
He moves on to the last job, which is to collect honey from the South American Bees. As soon as he starts, he is attacked by the bees. He grabs the spade and smashes the bees to a pulp. By now he knows what to do and throws them into the Lions cage.
Later that day a new Lion arrives at the zoo. He wanders up to another lion
and says "Alright pal. What's the food like here?"
The Lion replies, "Fucking brilliant mate, today we had Fish and Chimps with Mushy Bees."

We never hear anything from Rick Astley these days. It's almost like he's given us up, and let us down.

My cat somehow got into the washing machine, but at least it died in comfort.

I got really emotional at the petrol station this morning.
I don't know why, I just started filling up!

Today a man knocked on my door and asked for a small donation towards the local swimming pool.
So I gave him a glass of water.

Apparently, they're not making shortbread any longer....

Why are the Eiffel Tower lights so bright ?
French resistance is low.

My mum has had the same washing machine since my little brother Callum died 27 years ago...
I guess washing machines do live longer with Cal gone.

I bumped into Sheikh Mahand today... The world's friendliest Arab.

Back in the day everyone owned a horse, it was the rich that had cars.
Now everyone owns cars and it's the rich that have horses.
Oh my, how the stables have turned.

I can't believe no one has managed to come up with a cure for anorexia yet.
I thought it'd be a piece of cake.

BBC Breaking News:
The inventor of the anagram has died.... May he "erect a penis"....

I once dated a magazine collector. She had some issues.

Just walked down a street where the house numbers were 64K, 128K, 256K, 512K & 1MB.
Well, that was a trip down memory lane.

So much has changed since my girlfriend told me we're having a baby. For instance my name, address and telephone number!

I said to my wife, "I saw a woman with her tits out on the bus feeding her son."
She said, "It's natural."
"Natural?" I replied, "She was giving him crisps."

I've just invented a new word:
"Plagiarism"

When people describe it as raw sewage, is this so they don't get confused with cooked sewage?

Lewis Hamilton isn't the only F1 driver with a Scottish town in his name.
There's also..Stirling Moss, Eddie Irvine, Johnny Dumfries and Ayr toon centre.

I went for a job interview today and the manager said, 'We're looking for someone who is responsible.'
'Well, I'm your man', I replied, 'In my last job, whenever anything went wrong, they said I was responsible.'

My neighbours are listening to great music.
Whether they like it or not.

I bought my mother in law a chair for her 50th birthday but the wife won't let me plug it in.

Wife texts husband at work on a cold winters morning:
"Windows frozen."
Husband texts back:
"Pour some lukewarm water over it"
Wife texts back:
"Computer completely fucked now."

A man is walking home with his nine year old son, when the boy asks "Dad, what are those little boxes on the back of all those satellite dishes?
His father replies "Council houses son."

My mum always used to say "40 is the new 30". Lovely woman, banned from driving.

My neighbour knocked on my door at 2.30am, can you believe that, 2.30am?
Luckily for him I was still up playing my drums.

Can't believe my girlfriend just called me old fashioned. And with her ankles showing - the slut.

Just found out my uncle has left me a stately home in his will...I have no idea where Sod Hall is, I'm just off to Google it now!

Raising children is easy.
Just keep the boys away from the blue lights and girls from the red lights.

I remember when I took my son to the pub for the first time
I bought him a pint of bitter, he didn't like it so I drank it, I bought him a pint of lager, same thing, cider same thing, alcopops, same thing.
I bought him the full selection of spirits, he didn't like any of them so I had to finish them off, so we finally went home.
How the fuck I got that pushchair home I'll never know.

A woman from the local children's home knocked at our door earlier asking for a donation.
So I gave her my ginger stepson.

My mate fucking hates his surname, Potato.
Although not as much as his wife, Jackie does.

I just lost a good friend of mine in a terrible accident. He got his finger stuck in a wedding ring.

I looked outside and it was pissing it down. I thought, 'Fuck it, I'm not going out in that. I'll pick the kids up from school tomorrow.'

My mother in law has her funeral on Monday. My wife has asked me to buy some suitable gloves for the funeral.
Does anybody know where I can get them giant foam fingers from?

We were all sat down watching the footie last night when my youngest son said "Dad, I need to tell you something..........I'm gay"
Then my eldest son said "Dad, I need to tell you that I'm gay also"
I said "Fuck me, is there anyone in this household other than me, that likes shagging women"?
"I do Dad" replied my daughter.

University: just the same as being unemployed.
But your parents are proud of you.

My mother always used to say, "Give your food a rinse before you eat it."
Lovely woman, terrible sandwiches.

We cleared out my gran's flat this morning, sorted out the good stuff and put it on eBay, and then went to the estate agents to put her flat on the market.
She'll be well pissed off when she gets back from bingo.

It's funny how definitions have changed for parents over the years. Your child is not 'badly behaved and a bit thick', they've got ADHD.
They're not a 'sissy', they're born in the wrong body,
They're not an 'interfering, opinionated, annoying little cunt', they're a vegan.

Don't be ashamed of yourself.
That's your parents' job.

Was telling my friend how I should get a blind dog for the mother law,
Do you not mean a guide dog he replied.
Nah definitely blind if the dog sees her it will probably go for her throat.

BBC to stop free TV licences for the over 75's.
Sad to put Grandma in a home, but she's no longer any use to me.

My parents found a bag of ecstasy pills in my bedroom today.
My mum said, "Is there something you'd like to share with us?"
"Not really," I replied. "I've only got ten left."

My Dad always used to say, "We should embrace our mistakes".
Then he'd give me a Big Hug.

People say gambling ruins lives, but it brought our family closer... we now live in a one bedroom flat.

I hate it when new parents ask me who their baby looks like.
It was born 2 days ago, it looks like a fucking potato.

I found my first grey pubic hair today.
That's the last time I eat nana's trifle.

After my wife died, I couldn't even look at another woman for 10 years. But now that I'm out of jail, I can honestly say it was worth it!

Got an e-mail today from a "bored housewife 32, looking for some action!" I've sent her my ironing, that'll keep her busy.!

The wife's been hinting she wants something black and lacy for her birthday. So, I've got her a pair of football boots!

Growing up with a dyslexic father had its advantages. Whenever he caught me swearing, he used to wash my mouth out with soup.

My wife asked if she could have a little peace and quiet while she cooked the dinner, so I took the batteries out of the smoke alarm!

Anyone got an owner's manual for a wife? Mine's giving off a terrible whining noise!

My wife apologised for the first time ever today. She said she's sorry she ever married me!

My son was hooked up to all these machines and wires, and hadn't even moved for almost a week.
Finally I had enough and went and unplugged the wi-fi.

After years of failed attempts, my wife and I decided to have one last try at the Fertility Clinic.
As we walked from the car park, I thought it might help if I lightened the mood a bit.
Breaking into a jog, I shouted back... "last one in's a rotten egg"

When I was a kid my parents told me "never open the cellar door"
One day they went out , so I sneaked up to it and pushed it open and saw wonderful things I had never seen before .
Like grass, trees, the sun, the sky .

When I was a kid, my dad sat me down and showed me pictures of why I should always wear a condom.
Funny thing is, they were all just pictures of me.

"I can't believe this" my wife said tearfully. "My very first Mother's Day and not even a card."
"Be reasonable" I told her. "He's only 7 months old".

Dont you find all these jokes about obese people horrible
Don't you think they have enough on their plate?

My grandads motto was 'if at first you don't succeed, try try try again'
Lovely man. Worst Dignitas employee ever.

Tonight a friend asked if he could crash on my couch.
I had to explain to him I was married now and that's where I sleep.

My mate came round today and saw my new car on the driveway.
"Nice car, how many miles to the gallon do you get?" He asked.
I replied, "About five, my wife and son get the fucking rest."

When I asked my Gran what she wanted for her birthday, she replied, "The best present I could ask for is to be surrounded by my friends."
Well, we've just got back from the cemetery and she doesn't seem too happy.

I felt like a real gentlemen opening the door for the mother in law earlier.
Mind you I was doing 60mph at the time.

If you get a new job before you quit your old one, it's considered responsible.
But if you do that with your girlfriend, it's called "cheating."

I was installing a light in the loft today, when I slipped off a joist and put my foot right through the bedroom ceiling. Fucking scared the shit out of my wife.
I'm not surprised though, she kicked me out last October.

In divorce women have all the rights and men have all the lefts...
Left homeless.

Left penniless.
Left childless.
Left for another man.

I was close to tears when my ex-wife told me she was getting remarried.
I really do feel sorry for him.

My wife is leaving me as she said I was so nosey.
Anyway, that's what was written in her diary.

I asked my wife to mark on the calendar the days she's on her period.
So I can stand silently in a corner and pray she doesn't make eye contact.

"Mr. Clark, I have reviewed this case very carefully," the divorce court judge said, "And I've decided to give your wife 775 pounds a week."
"That's very fair, your honour." the husband said "And every now and then I'll try to send her a few quid myself!".

I keep my former wife locked in a cupboard for entertainment.
It's my ex box.

My ex used to beat me senseless with her stringed instruments.
If only I had known about her history of violins.

My wife left me a note saying she had left me because of my poor eyesight.
I cant see why she did that.

My mate texted me and asked what I was doing.
"Probably failing my driving test," I replied.

My email password has been hacked again.
That's the third time I've had to rename the cat.

A photographer went to a dinner party. The host says, "I love your pictures, you must have a good camera." After the party the photographer says to the host, "That was a lovely meal, you must have a good stove."

I asked my girlfriend to get me a newspaper.
"Don't be silly," she replied, "you can use my Ipad."
That spider never knew what fucking hit it.

Why is it that all instruments created to find "intelligent life" are pointed "AWAY" from Earth

I changed my computer password to "incorrect."
So it automatically reminds me if I enter it wrong.

In a survival situation, you can drink your own urine.
Fortunately the wifi came back on as I was filling the can.

I love it when the clocks go forward.
It means when I'm having sex, I last for 1 hour and 30 seconds. I like this!

I got sacked from PC World today. A guy came in the store and asked me what was the best thing to finding your ancestors, and I said a shovel.

As of midnight last night if we laid all the people on Facebook end to end around the world, three quarters of them would have drowned

I went to my girlfriend's funeral today.
It was the first time I'd met her parents.
What a pair of miserable bastards.

School rang me today and said, "Your son's been telling lies"....
I replied, "Well tell him he's fucking good at it - I haven't got a son"....

When I was a kid, I can remember me mam going to the shops with two shillings in her purse and coming back with a big bag of spuds, two loaves of bread, a pound of cheese, three pints of milk, half a dozen eggs and a packet of tea.

You can't do that anymore,
Too many fucking security cameras.

I had a lucky escape today, I was watching the news on tv and my 8 year old came in from his first day at a new school "what's a wanker dad" he asked well I wasn't quite sure what to say when all of a sudden Jeremy Corbyn came on tv and saved the day.

My wife and I have decided to go down the adoption route and have discussed our preferences. She wants a girl and I want a Snow Leopard.

Just got a new job and my mum asked me, "What sort of hours are you doing?"
I said, "Sixty minute ones, you thick woman."

My young son proudly showed me his finger painting when he came home from school earlier:
"That's absolutely shit" I said, "it looks nothing like a finger."

A woman pregnant with her first child paid a visit to her obstetrician's office. After the exam, she shyly said "My husband wants me to ask you…" The doctor interrupts "I know… I know…" placing a reassuring hand on her shoulder, "I get asked that all the time. Sex is fine until late in the pregnancy." "No, that's not it…" the woman confessed. "He wants to know if I can still mow the lawn."

My wife and I are thinking of having a baby. We've always wondered what it must be like to live with an insomniac bagpipe player with dysentery.

In the News: 'Anti-natalist', 27, vows to SUE parents for giving birth to him without his consent as he compares all births to 'kidnap and slavery'.
I would also like to sue his parents, for giving birth to a dick!

"She's lovely", said my wife.
"She's at that age where she can almost sit up on her own, and we don't get too many soiled nappies."

"When she gurgles and blows raspberries it sounds almost like she's talking."
She adores her Mum!

The other day at home my 8 year son came running in from school all excited
"Dad! Dad!" he shouted "I've just been picked for a major part in the school play"
"Really Son?" I said " That's brilliant, what's it about"
"Well Dad, It's all about family life and I'm playing the part of a man who's been married for 25 years"
"Never mind Son" I said "Maybe next time you'll get a speaking part!"

I totally failed Safety and Health course today...
How did you manage to do that?
Well, one of the questions was, "in the event of a fire, what steps would you take?"
And?
"Fucking large ones" was apparently the wrong answer.

forward
comment filter_none thumb_up_alt more_horiz
Joke by Simmoblade in Other - Parent · 3 Y
Enjoyed a lovely Father's Day meal today, washed down with a nice couple of pints, but all my wife and kids have done is moan about it.
And then they wonder why I didn't take them with me

Mother - "the headmaster tells me you've been expelled for use the c - word in class?"
"That wasn't clever was it?"
Son - "no it was cunt"

By the time the car had finished rolling I realised my mother had given me bad advice.
"Wear clean underwear in case you have an accident" was a waste of fucking time.

Met the girlfriends parents for the first time last week, they said "our home is your home. So I sold it ..

Why do farts smell daddy ?
For the benefit of the deaf son.

After many months of agonising, I finally had to put my dad in a care home.
After a few weeks I gave the home a ring to find out how he was.
The nurse told me "Well I'm afraid he is a bit like a fish out of water"
"What, having trouble settling in is he"? I asked
"No, he's dead"! she replied.

What do you call a non binary parent that only wears see through clothes?
A Trans-parent.

Told the girlfriend that Mum is deaf so speak loud and slow.
Told Mum that the girlfriend is retarded.

A charity worker stopped me in the street and asked if I fancied taking part in a marathon. I was going to decline but he told me it was for disabled kids and children with severe learning difficulties.
I thought, fuck me, I might win this.

My therapist told me that a great way to let go of your anger is to write letters to people you hate and then burn them.
I did that and I feel much better but I am wondering do I keep the letters.?

At the barbers today, I asked to have my hair cut like Tom Cruise. So he gave me a cushion to sit on.

My driving instructor told me, NEVER brake if there's an animal in the road.
You should have seen the look on the copper's face as I knocked him off his horse.

Just got a copy of Pirates of the Caribbean and I'm taking it back. I put the disc in and the first thing it told me was that it was illegal to watch pirate movies.

My wife has left me because of my terrible Arnold Schwarzenegger impression
But don't worry.......... I'll return

At the National Gallery a husband and wife were staring at a portrait that had them completely confused.
The painting depicted three black men totally naked sitting on a park bench. Two of the figures had black penises, but the one in the middle had a pink penis.
The curator of the gallery realized that they were having trouble interpreting the painting and offered his assessment.
He went on for over half an hour explaining how it depicted the sexual emasculation of black men in a predominately white, patriarchal society. 'In fact,' he pointed out, 'some serious critics believe that the pink penis also reflects the cultural and sociological oppression experienced by gay men in contemporary society.'
After the curator left, a man approached the couple and said, 'Would you like to know what the painting is really about?'
'Now why would you claim to be more of an expert than the curator of the gallery?' asked the couple.
'Because I'm the man who painted it,' he replied.
'In fact, there are no black men depicted at all! They're just three Welsh coal miners. The guy in the middle went home for lunch.

McDonald's were giving away 18-month old, badly behaved, kids and 10 Mayfair fags to any white girl in a tracksuit aged between 12 and 15 yesterday.
Or so it seemed.

I'm so proud of my Ethiopian pen pal.
He tells me he hasn't had a drink in weeks. Hang in there mate.

I lost the bar trivia contest last night by one point. The last question was, "Where do women have the curliest hair?" Apparently the correct answer is, Fiji.

Our young son has been crying a lot at night, so my wife asked me to go out and get a baby monitor for him.
But he seems even more freaked out now with the big lizard crawling all over him.

I don't usually brag about my finances, but my credit card company calls me almost every day to tell me my balance is outstanding

One of my mates told me that I often make people uncomfortable by violating their personal space.
It was an incredibly hurtful thing to say and completely ruined our bath.

A woman stopped me in the street this morning and asked if I'd ever considered changing my energy provider.
I said, "No, I'm quite happy with food."

I was just viewing a woman's profile on a dating website,
'Blonde 33 From London Great Personality 5ft 3 Green Eyes.'
Don't get me wrong, I got nothing against short women, but, 3 green eyes?
No wonder she's single.

I've just seen the most confusing book.
Ventriloquism for Dummies

My wife asked me to put tomato ketchup on the shopping list that I was writing out.
I can't read a fucking word now.

I cannot believe that in this day and age that wearing underwear in the garden would offend so many people...admittedly it wasn't my garden or my underwear.

My girlfriend isn't talking to me because apparently I ruined her birthday.
I'm not sure how I did that – I didn't even know it was her birthday...

I got a right slap across the face yestreday.
I got into a lift (elevator for our colonial friends), and this busty woman followed me in and I couldn't stop staring at her big tits.
Then she said "Would you mind pressing 1 for me"
I must say, the slap was worth it.

Me and the mrs were watching crimewatch and they were talking about a bank robbery that had taken place. They showed a picture of one of the suspects and said "Have you seen this man?"
I phoned up the hotline but apparently "No" wasn't the answer they were looking for

My wife and I were so proud of our daughter standing in front of us after trying on her Wedding Dress.
"Give us a twirl," said my wife.
The proudest moment of my life and all that fat bitch wants is chocolate!

Proof that woman do things just to start an argument.
My misses rang me at work today and said "I've not had time to start tea, do you fancy going out for some".
"yeah that sounds good" I replied.
When I got home from the restaurant there she was sat at the kitchen table with a face like thunder.

A businessman is away from home for a few days on a sales conference, he plans to take full advantage of his few days of freedom and has Googled the numbers of female escorts in the locality. He picks up the bedside telephone and pudgy fingers punch in the first of the numbers, he waits, he hears a young female voice answer, "Listen, I want you to come to my Hotel room for a couple of hours, I want oral, I want to do anal and I want to jizz all over your

tits!"
There is a pause and the young woman replies, "That sounds like great fun but you need to dial 9 to get an outside line Sir."

This girl gave me a wink in the pub last night and asked if I'd like to go to her place and see her beaver.
Odd animal to keep as a pet.

I went to the the local library for a book, I asked the lady for a book on Psycho the Rapist, she said, i think its pronounced Psychotherapist.

I had a job interview last night for a job as a Blacksmith
The person interviewing me asked
"Have you ever shoed a horse before"
I replied
"No but I once told a Donkey to Fuck off if that's any help"

I rang Ryanair to book a flight.
The woman at the other end said "How many will be flying with you"?
I replied "How the bloody hell should I know?, it's your fucking aeroplane"

I saw a woman drop her purse in the high street this morning, so I quickly followed her.
As I was just about to tap her on the shoulder she started running for a bus.
So I ran after her shouting, "You dropped your purse! You dropped your purse!"
She didn't hear me and proceeded to get onto the bus, so I got on the bus too.
As I walked to the back of the bus I breathlessly said, "You dropped your purse on the floor outside McDonald's."
"Thank you so much" she said, "Where is it?"
I said, "I've just fucking told you, on the floor outside McDonald's."

I'll never understand women, my wife said to me earlier:

"Babe, I'm stuck on 6 across. 8 letters, fixed the highway?"
"Retarred." I replied.
Ungrateful bitch just threw the paper at me and stormed out.

My mates called me a tight arse. So I decided to buy them a beer to prove I'm not.
Turns out they wanted one each.

I saw a poster that read, 'Not all disabilities are visible.'
I don't know about you, but I reckon being invisible would be more of a superpower than a disability.

I'm so excited that this girl said I was the one! I'm sure the other guys in the police lineup are jealous.

My father always told me to keep a cricket bat under my bed for protection.
Turned out to be substantially less effective than condoms.

My boss said I should dress for the job I want, not for the job I have.... Long story short I'm sat in a disciplinary meeting dressed as Batman

BBC News: Police hold teenage girl over fire in London...
Bit harsh!

One of my mates told me that I often make people uncomfortable by violating their personal space.
Which was an incredibly unnecessary and hurtful thing to say. It ruined our bath.

One of the most awkward things that can happen in a pub is when your pint-to-toilet cycle gets synchronised with a complete stranger.

I came downstairs this morning to a note on the fridge from my girlfriend.
It said, 'I can't live like this anymore, John. I'm leaving you. It's clearly not working.'
Well I don't know what the fuck she's talking about.

The milk is still cold and the light comes on when you open the door.

Man in hospital bed wearing an oxygen mask over his mouth. 'Nurse', he mumbles. 'Are my testicles black?'
Nurse raises his gown, holds his penis in one hand and his testicles in the other. She takes a close look and says 'There's nothing wrong with them, sir'.
Man pulls off the oxygen mask, smiles at her and says very slowly, 'Thanks for that, it was lovely......but listen very carefully. Are-my-test-results-back ???'

Just mentioned to the missus that I've always had a bit of a thing for Beyoncé.
"Whatever floats your boat". She said.
"No" I said, "that's buoyancy".

My mate's just moved, so I got him a set of radiators...
It's a house-warming present.

I work with a Chinese guy called Kim and one time at a works function, we were having a drink and I said to him "Do you ever get fed up of us Westerners saying that all Chinese people look the same"?
He replied "Kim's at the bar getting drinks, I'm his wife"

A man hates his wife"s cat so much he drives to the next town and dumps it.
When he gets home, it"s there.
Next day he drives 50 miles and dumps it.
When he gets home, it"s there.
So the next day he drives to the other side of the country and dumps it.
One hour later he rings his wife and asks, "is the cat home?"
"Yes, why?" asks his wife."
Put the cunt on," he says, "I"m fucking lost."

A mother takes her four year old daughter into the bank and the little girl goes up to the counter and says " as I now have a job I would like to open a bank account" the manager replies oh what sort of a job do you have?" The little girl replies " I have a job on a building site" the mother explains that they have builders working on land at the bottom of their garden and the builders have taken a shine to her daughter and let her turn the hose on and off and as she has been so helpful have given her a proper pay packet. " well that's wonderful says the bank manager it's so good to work hard and receive a pay packet, are you working next week?" " yes says the little girl if those cunts from Jewson deliver the fucking bricks on time."

I was staying in a hotel last night. I phoned down to reception.
"Hi, this is room 26 Can I have a wake up call , please?"
She said "Yes, You're in your mid 30s, single , live with your mother and have achieved nothing in life !"

It really annoys me when people put swear words at the end of their joke just to make it funny.
Cunts.

Two businessmen in the centre of London were sitting down for a break in their soon-to-be new store. As yet, the store wasn't ready, with only a few shelves set up.
One said to the other, "I bet any minute now some pensioner is going to walk by, put their face to the window, and ask what we're selling." No sooner were the words out of his mouth when, sure enough, a curious old woman walked to the window, had a peek, and in a soft voice asked, "What are you selling here?"
One of the men replied sarcastically, "We're selling arseholes."
Without skipping a beat, the old woman said,"Must be doing well...Only two left.!"

I'm setting up a help group for bike riders who ignore red lights. Please fell free to join Cyclists Unable to Notice Traffic Signals.

Ireland has had its worst ever air disaster. A small 4-seater plane has crashed into a Cemetary.

So far, rescue workers have retrieved 432 bodies but expect the number to rise as digging continues through the night

I had a job at a Cadbury's factory putting fudge bars in to boxes. I had to quit though because every time someone would walk past they would say,
"Oh packing fudge are we?" Or "Hey up, he's packing fudge again."
Since then I've applied for a job in a clothing factory lifting boxes of shirts.
I'm hoping the name calling will stop now.

I was talking to a girl in the bar last night.
She said, "If you lost a few pounds, had a shave and got your hair cut, you'd look all right."
I said, "If I did that, I'd be talking to your friends over there instead of you."

Whats the definition of Irony?
Size 22 Skinny jeans.

Piers Morgan picked up the phone one day and a voice said "Is that Piers Morgan"?
He replied "Yes, can I help you"?
The voice then said " Well, I hope so, you see I came into an office stationary outlet and asked for a Dictaphone and they gave me your number"

Me and my girlfriend stopped at the motorway services recently for some breakfast.
We got two fry ups, two coffees and two jam doughnuts. I got to the cashier and I said, "I'm sorry, love, but I only have a £50 note."
"That's okay," she said, "just put the doughnuts back."

I said to the baker.. "How come all your cakes are 50p and that one's £1"
He said..." that's Madeira cake"

The mother in law came for Sunday dinner, and while sitting at

the table she moaned,
"Why is the dog sitting here on the floor staring at me?"
I replied, "you're using his plate".

Just saw a sign that made me piss myself.....
Toilets Closed.

First rule of Vegan club.
Tell fucking everyone about Vegan club.

While the wife was in the kitchen cooking breakfast I suddenly heard a loud thud. Running in I found her collapsed on the floor & not breathing. I was in a blind frenzy, I had no idea what to do. Then i remembered, Wetherspoons do an all day breakfast for just £3.99

Alcohol...Because sometimes the truth needs a laxative.

After finding 5 Mars bars, 3 Snickers, a Flake and a packet of M&M's, I'm starting to think I'm not cut out to be a Bounty hunter....

Are you tired of boiling water every time you make pasta? Boil a few gallons at the beginning of the week and freeze it for later.

The wife came home with 4 bottles of whisky, 3 boxes of wine, 3 crates of beer and 2 loaves of bread.
"Are we expecting company?" I asked.
"No," she replied.
"Then why did you buy so much fucking bread."

I left a packet of Quorn at the supermarket checkout today.
I went back and asked the assistant, "Have you seen my vegetarian mince ?"
She said, "No, but walk up and down that aisle and I'll give you my honest opinion"

BBC health news: "So-called 'healthy option' pre-packed sandwiches contain more salt than a bag of walkers crisps."
Probably contain more crisps, too.

What do we want
A cure for obesity
When do we want it
After tea

I said to a Policeman "If I called you a cunt would you arrest me?
The Policeman replied "Yes I would arrest you"
I said "What if I was just thinking you're a cunt"?
"There's not much I can do about that" he replied
"Good" I said, "Because I think you're a cunt"!

The boss of Ryanair, Michael O'Leary, walks into a Dublin bar and orders a pint of Guinness. The Landlord says, "That'll be one €uro please Mr O'Leary." O'Leary replies, "You're a man after me own heart, do you know all the other bars around here charge five €uros for a pint of Guinness?" The Landlord responds, "I have to be honest Mr O'Leary I took a leaf out of your book, slashed the cost of everything and business is booming." O'Leary hands over one €uro with a smile, the Landlord asks, "Will you be wanting a glass with your Guinness sir ?"

I wonder if my Vets receptionist realises how many peoples passwords she knows?

Paddy took 2 stuffed dogs to the Antiques Roadshow.
The presenter said, "This is a very rare set, produced by the celebrated Johns Brothers taxidermists who operated in London at the turn of the last century.
Do you have any idea what they would fetch if they were in good condition?"
"Sticks!" Paddy replied

Due to the water shortage in Ireland, Dublin Swimming Baths have announced that they are closing lanes 7 and 8.

I phoned my local radio station today.
When the guy answered the phone he said, "Congratulations on being our 1st caller, all you have to do is answer the next question

correctly to win our grand prize."
"Wahoo!" I shouted in delight.
"It's a Maths question," he said. "Feeling confident?"
"I've got a degree in Maths and I teach it at my local school," I proudly replied.
"Okay then, to win 2 VIP tickets to see Justin Bieber and to meet him back stage afterwards, what's 2+2?"
"7," I replied.

My mate went to get a tattoo of an Indian on his back. Half way through he said, "Don't forget to put a big tomahawk in his hand." The tattooist said "For fuck sake, give us a chance mate, I've only just finished his turban!"

Four teens arrested in Bury St Edmunds after they chucked flour and eggs on a disabled woman and posed for sickening photos.
The victim is being comforted at the local hostel for battered women.

A bra designer for Playtex has designed a new bra that stops women's tits from bouncing up and down and stops the nipples from poking out when they are cold.
His work colleagues took him outside and kicked the shit out of him.

Congrats to all those getting their A levels today. To all those going on to uni to do art or multimedia, just remember one thing. I don't want pickles on my big mac.

Men with beards 50 years ago: "I'm going to the woods to chop down some trees."
Men with beards today: "I'm going to the shops there's a new face mask that's gluten-free."

Twas the night before Christmas
And all through the house
Not a creature was stirring
Except for a Scouse

He's in through your window
He's out with a sack
To take to his dealer
To swop for some crack

I've just found out that the chippy in Sellafield has closed down. What a shame, they used to serve a lovely leg of cod there.

Why did the vegan cross the road?
To tell someone they were a vegan.

What did one Walkers crisp say to the other?
Nothing they were in two different packets.

Man walks into an appliance store and goes up to the cashier
Have you any two-watt bulbs?
For what?
That'll do. I'll take two.
Two what?
I thought you didn't have any.
Any what?

"This next song is about subtraction."
"Take it away boys."

i, for one, like roman numerals.

I was out fishing yesterday when I heard a soft voice saying "Kiss me, then I will turn into your faithful mistress"
I looked down and saw a little frog, " I said "Was that you speaking"?
The little frog said "Yes, kiss me and I will turn into your faithful mistress"
So I picked the little frog up and placed it in an empty bait box.
When I got home, the missus was out, so I opened the bait box and the little frog said "Are you going to kiss me now so I can turn into your faithful mistress"?
I said "Nah, at my age I'd rather have a talking frog"

If you say "gullible" really slowly, it sounds like lemons.

When I go to someone's house and they tell me to make myself at home, the first thing I do is throw them out because I don't like visitors.

My girlfriend says I'm hopeless at fixing appliances.
Well, she's in for a shock.

I saw a £50 note just lying on the pier In Brighton today.
But I decided it wasn't worth risking bending over to pick it up...

A chap goes to the Council for a job. The interviewer asks him - "Have you been in the armed services?" Yes" he says "I was in the Falklands for three years." The interviewer says "That will give you extra points toward employment" and then asks "Are you disabled in any way?" The guy says "Yes 100%... a land mine blew my testicles off." The interviewer tells the guy "OK. I can hire you right now. The hours are from 8:00 AM. to 4:00 PM You can start tomorrow. Come in at 10:00AM ." The guy is puzzled and says "If the hours are from 8:00AM to 4:00 PM why do you want me to come in at 10:00 AM? " "This is a council job" the interviewer replies. "For the first two hours we sit around scratching our balls...no point in you coming in for that..........

Jokes on you, I got my degree in gender studies while there were still only two of them.

A 12 year old boy gets hit by a car at a busy intersection.
A woman witnesses the entire event and runs over to the little boy, who's lying on the ground in a pool of blood.
She gently cradles the boy's head in her arms and whispers, "Do you need a priest?"
The boy moans, "How you can think of sex at a time like this?"

I was Talking to a transgender person recently but it was really distracting because he was wearing a really short skirt.
To be honest that showed some balls.

Why call it boob sweat?
And not humidititties?

Male menopause is a lot more fun than female menopause. With female menopause you gain weight and get hot flushes.
Male menopause - you get to date young girls and ride motorcycles.

I was a test tube baby.
My star sign is Pyrex

Pansexual? I have never been sexually attracted to pans, but I did think that the stove was hot.

There's a redhead, a brunette and a blonde in the hospital maternity ward all ready to give birth.
The redhead says "I'm going to have a boy because my husband was on top during conception and my Gran told me that this is how you can determine the gender of your baby"
The brunette says "I'm going to have a girl then if that's the case, because my husband was underneath during conception"
The blonde thinks for a moment and says "Oh no! it looks like I'm going to have puppies"!

You can tell the gender of an ant by putting it on water.
If it sinks, Girl ant.
If it floats, Bouyant.

On a form now, when I'm asked what my sex is - Male, Female, Other - under 'Other', I put 'H2O'.
I'm gender fluid.

The saddest day for a coach is when your team folds. With regret I announce the end of the Nags Head Ladies FC 2nd eleven.
Following Samira Ahmed's pay gap victory against the BBC, the girls all wanted to be paid the same as as Lionel Messi.

How many men does it take to mop a floor?
None. It's a woman's job.

Apparently on average one person in a group of males is gay.
I think it's Dave myself, he's super cute

I'm not racialist or nothing but I had to give up my job as a scaffolder because there were too many poles.

I was grilling a steak earlier and the smell of the juices started to make my mouth water...
Got me thinking, do vegans get the same reaction when mowing the lawn?

Have YOU had to walk 500 miles?
Were you advised to walk 500 more?
You could be entitled to compensation.
Call the Pro Claimers NOW.

Buy your Vegan friend a Venus Flytrap and show them even plants think they're wrong.

I went to a vegetarian restaurant and the waiter asked, "How was your meal, sir?"
"It was very nice. My compliments to the gardener."

If god hadn't intended us to eat animals, he wouldn't have made them out of food.

"Now, Madam, can you describe the man who stole your handbag?"
"Oh, it all happened so fast! He pushed me over from behind, I didn't see him at all. One thing though; he was a vegan."
"How do you know that?"
"He fucking told me as he was running off."

Marks & Spencer apologised for switching the labels on some of their salads.
Apparently the mistake caused vegans to accidentally eat chicken.
So if you're a vegan and you ate one of M&S salads, that's why it was so yummy.

I knocked a proud to be vegan cyclist off his bike today after he went through a red light. I've had to bill him for damage to my car, the police and ambulance services attended but I've been assured by the paramedic despite the cyclist having broken bones I will eventually stop laughing.

Why did the vegan cross the road?
To tell someone that they are a vegan.

I went to a vegan restaurant once. Wait, no, that was just a florist.

What's the best way to quit being vegan?
Cold turkey.

I've been told by a vegan that I should grow my food, not hunt it. Does anyone know how to grow bacon?

I've decided to show my support for Vegans.
From now on, I'll only wear leather from cows fed on grass.

Greggs are launching a Vegan sausage roll. There is no meat in it. They are calling it....
A Sausage Roll.

I only eat vegan. They're easy to catch and don't put up much of a fight.

I couldn't believe it when this vegan activist got in my face yesterday and stated waving a flyer at me.
She kept going on about, "All the cows and their cow flatulence is destroying the ozone layer," and stuff like this... and then she finally glared right at me and said, "And what are YOU doing about it ?"
I quickly replied, "I'm eating the cows."

My dyslexic vegetarian Muslim neighbour stoned his wife to death yesterday.
All she did was tell him she'd burned the Quorn.

I recently met a level five vegan.

She doesn't eat anything that casts a shadow.

"We're going to have to switch off your wife's life support," said the doc, "she's in a vegan state."
"Don't you mean vegetative?" I asked.
"No, vegan," he replied, "if it was vegetative there'd at least be some hope."

Sometimes I wonder how vegans can survive off what little they can eat,
then I remember they just feed off attention.

A friend sent me a card congratulating me for doing Veganuary.
Thanks, tastiest thing I've eaten so far.

Phrases like 'bring home the bacon' and 'take the bull by the horns' are offensive to vegans.
Well, I don't like being full of beans or going bananas - but do you hear me moan?

A vegan girl just posted a picture of a cow on Facebook, she'd written underneath, "How do you eat these poor, defenceless animals.."
I replied, "I can't speak for everyone, but personally, I like mine with, mixed veg, tatties and gravy..."

Homosexuals and mentally disabled people are the staple diet of vegan cannibals.
Fruits and veg.

Why did the chicken cross the road?
To tell someone it's a vegan.

What's the hardest part of making a vegan pizza?
Skinning the vegan.

Invited by vegetarians for dinner? Point out that since you`d no doubt be made aware of their special dietary requirements, tell them about yours, and ask for a nice steak.

I'll never forget the couple of days that my wife tried to turn vegetarian.
I knew it wouldn't last, as usually grazing brontosauruses look much happier.

How do you know if a complete stranger happens to be a vegan?
They'll tell you

New Scientist magazine reports about a new study. Apparently men who are vegan have a much lower sperm count compared to those that eat meat.
And the few sperm vegan men do have ... want nothing to do with eggs anyway.

F - FACE: Has it fallen on one side?
A - ARMS: Can they raise them?
S - SPEECH: Is it slurred?
T - TIME... to get her knickers down. The rohypnol has kicked in.

The Car of the Year for 2020, as voted by Woman magazine is:
A Blue one.

The guy sat next to me on the train pulled out a photo of his wife and said, "She's beautiful, isn't she?" I said, "If you think she's beautiful, you should see my girlfriend mate."
He said, "Why? Is she a stunner?" I said, "No, she's an optician."

My mate just said, "What's your favorite mythical creature?"
I said, "Those happy women in tampax adverts."

The Mrs has left me because I'm too insecure....
No, wait she's back....
She was just making a cup of tea....

I saw a woman driver cause an accident today.
She indicated that she was turning right and then actually fucking turned right.

Women are the only creatures to defy the laws of gravity.

The heavier they are, the easier they are to pick up.

A scientist has invented a bra that stops tits bobbing up and down and nipples sticking out in the cold.
His colleagues have kicked his fucking head in!

"If you win the lottery the first thing I want you to buy me is a boob job and facelift" said my 49 yr old girlfriend as I was checking my numbers last night,
"Well actually the first things I would get is a reconditioned engine and a respray for my Mondeo" I replied
"Why bother tarting that old thing up, you might as well get a new one" she retorted
"My point exactly"

Women deserve equal rights.
And lefts.

Women are a lot like video games.
When they get too difficult, you have to cheat.

I've just heard the official song for the England women's football world cup team.
Steam irons on a shirt.

Stalking is when two people go for a long romantic walk together but only one of them knows it

Words cannot describe how beautiful you are.
But numbers can, 6 / 10.

I'd like to thank the girl with no sports bra who ran with me through the last few miles of yesterday's marathon.
Your lack of support got me through.

A recent survey says that 15% of the nations women are taking medication for mental illness.
bloody hell, that could only mean the other 85% are walking around untreated.

Element Name: Woman
Periodic Chart Symbol: Wo
Discoverer: Adam
Atomic Mass: Generally accepted as 110 lbs., but known to vary from 60 to 550 lbs.
Occurrence: Copious quantities in all urban areas.

PHYSICAL PROPERTIES
1. Surface usually covered with a painted film.
2. Boils with no provocation.
3. Freezes up solid unexpectedly.
4. Melts if given special treatment.
5. Bitter if incorrectly used or ignored.
6. Yields to pressure applied to certain points.

CHEMICAL PROPERTIES
1. Has a great affinity for gold, silver, platinum and precious stones such as diamonds, rubies and sapphires among others.
2. Absorbs great quantities of expensive substances.
3. May explode spontaneously without prior warning or reason.
4. Insoluble in liquids, but activity greatly increased by saturation in alcohol.
5. Most powerful money-reducing agent known to man.

COMMON USES
1. Highly ornamental, especially in sports car.
2. Can be a great aid to relaxation.
3. Very effective cleaning agent.

TESTS
1. Pure specimen turns rosy pink when discovered in the natural state.
2. Turns green with envy when placed beside a better specimen.
3. Defies proper ageing analysis techniques.

HAZARDS
1. Highly dangerous except in experienced hands.
2. Illegal to possess more than one at a time although several can be maintained at different locations as long as the specimens do not come into contact with each other.

Due to an unfortunate genetic defect, I have been told that I can't drive. It has left me with a lack of spatial awareness, an inability to think logically and terrible mood swings.
On the upside, I can have kids, I'm great at housework and I've got a cracking set of tits.

The wizard of Oz.
A film about two women fighting over a pair of shoes.

I walked up to a girl in the pub and asked her if she liked the strong and silent type.
"As a matter of fact I do." She said.
So I let out a fart and walked away.

After almost a year in a coma my wife is having to learn the basics again.
How to walk, how to talk, How to feed herself and How to not argue with me at the top of the stairs again.

My wife crashed her car this morning.
When the police came she said the guy involved was on his mobile and eating a pie at the time. The police advised her the guy was entitled to do what he wanted in his own conservatory.

I dunno why women are always bragging about being able to multi-task.
It's really just a side effect of their complete inability to make up their mind

Why are women so good in hockey?
Because it looks so much like vacuuming!

Married women are more fulfilled with their lives than single women, a new study shows...
Or vice versa, depending on their mood.

My girlfriend accused me of "Cheating on her".
I thought to myself: "She's beginning to sound just like my Wife".

The women's trophy for winning Wimbledon is essentially just a plate, just to remind them what they should be doing instead of playing tennis.
f
A man loses both his ears in a freak accident, the surgeon tells him he can replace them with two new fully transplanted ears, and they have a donor ready.
A few days later the bandages are removed and amazingly he can hear everything crystal clear.
But as the day goes on he realises somethings not right.
He says to the doc "I can hear, but just don't seem to understand anything now"
The doc says "I'm sorry sir that's because those ears once belonged to a woman"

Women are finally being allowed to join the SAS.
About time as well, there's no way those brave lads should be cooking their own meals.

Fairy liquid's ads have been updated to reflect modern England.
"Mummy why are your hands so soft?"
"Cos i'm only 14 innit, now shut the F*ck up and eat your pot noodle before your dad gets home from school."

I saw this girl crying in a pub, so I went up to her and asked what was wrong.
"I split up with my boyfriend, because he's a sexist pig."
"I'm a great listener, if you want to tell me more," I replied.
"You don't even know me," she cried, "why would you want to listen to me?"
"Because you have massive tits."

My girlfriend dumped me because of my obsession with plants.
I asked "Where's this stemming from petal?"

I fucking hate it when couples have a little argument and the girlfriend changes her facebook status to 'single'

I mean, I have arguments with my parents all the time and you don't see me changing my status to 'orphan'.

Is it just me or has the increase in female MPs coincided with parliament not fucking listening?

My late Mother-in-law is famous for her 9 dart finish.
The pygmies said they'd never killed anything that big before.

Had the mother in law round for lunch today. My dog sat right at her feet, gazing up adoringly at her. She said, "That's so cute, is he really that fond of me?" I said, "No, it's just that you're eating off his plate."

How to make a woman mad in Two simple steps:
1.take a picture of her
2.don't show her.

Can we all just stop telling women to get back in the kitchen? There's laundry to be done, too.

A lot of men objectify women.
Not me, I think they're great things.

Christmas is coming so be careful on the roads as quite a lot of guys will be having a few drinks and letting their wives drive

The CIA had an opening for an assassin. After all of the background checks, interviews, and testing were done, there were three finalists: two men and one woman. For the final test, the CIA agents took one of the men to a large metal door and handed him a gun.
"We must know that you will follow your instructions, no matter what the circumstances. Inside this room you will find your wife sitting in a chair. You have to kill her."
The first man said, "You can't be serious. I could never shoot my wife."
The agent replies, "Then you're not the right man for this job."
The second man was given the same instructions. He took the gun and went into the room. All was quiet for about five minutes.

Then the agent came out with tears in his eyes. "I tried, but I can't kill my wife."
The agent replies, "You don't have what it takes. Take your wife and go home."
Finally, it was the woman's turn. Only she was told to kill her husband. She took the gun and went into the room. Shots were heard, one shot after another. They heard screaming, crashing, banging on the walls. After a few minutes, all was quiet. The door opened slowly and there stood the woman. She wiped the sweat from her brow and said, "You guys didn't tell me the gun was loaded with blanks. I had to beat him to death with the chair."

"Watch the first all-female spacewalk."
Hours of two women refusing to talk to each other for wearing the same outfit. In slow-motion.

My girlfriend's leaving me because she says I'm a rubbish mime.
It must of been something I said.

A stunning blonde dressed in nothing more than a thong and a negligee, lets the plumber in.
"Hello, is your husband not in?" He asked.
"Does it look like he's in?" She replied opening her negligee, "will I not do?"
"Well not really" he said, "I need your car reversing out of the drive."

I got invited to A Day without Women lecture...
but I am not going because there won't be any coffee or sandwiches.

I was sat in traffic this morning, with the music blaring and in my own world. I noticed a few motorists in their cars pointing and laughing at something, so I turned the music down to see what was going on, I looked to my right and saw a naked woman with duck tape round her mouth, her feet and hands were tied up with cable tyres and was hopping like mad along the pavement. Me and the other motorists were hysterical. However, the laughs soon turned to sheer panic, as I looked in my interior mirror and noticed the boot of the car was open...

My wife looked out of the window and said it's not going to stop is it?
"Of course it fucking isn't", I shouted, "You didn't put the handbrake on!"

My wife took her car in for a service on Sunday.
"It's the first time we've ever seen anyone crash their vehicle into a church," said the shaken parishioners.

Astrology: because millions of planets and stars have spent billions of years lining themselves up just to let her know that she'll "meet someone with nice eyes today."

Following the birth of her fifth child, resulting in a front bottom that resembled a torn out fireplace rather than a tidy taco shell, the woman decided to get labiaplasty.
She expressly asked that nobody be made aware of her vanity and keep the surgery quiet.
Upon waking from her surgery, the lady spotted three long stemmed roses at the foot of her bed. She called the nurse over to ask who knew about her surgery and why they sent roses.
The nurse said that the first rose was from the surgeon, to thank her for being such a model patient.
The second one was from her husband who wishes her well and can't wait to see her home again.
Who was the third one from? Asked the woman.
Oh, that's from little Timmy down on the burns ward. He's thanked you for his new ears.

Apple Products have just announced the development of a device that fits inside women's breast implants and plays hi-fideliity music.
The iTit, (it's market name), will cost from £399 to £499 depending on speaker size.
This would be a major breakthrough, as women have always com-

plained that men spend more time looking at their tits rather than listening to them.

The police phoned me to tell me my wife was in hospital.
"How is she?" I asked.
"Very critical," replied the officer.
"What's she fucking complaining about now?" I said.

My wife is in hospital after being beaten up for using the 'N' word. Next time I ask for a beer from the fridge, she had better use the 'Y' word.

Me and the wife have just been to the cinema to see that film Suffragette.
Two hours of a woman's struggle........full of tears, aggression, sadness, anger and frustration.
Anyway, after she finally managed to park the car in the cinema car park we rushed in and caught the credits...

"You're so childish" screamed the wife. "Why do you always have to use that stupid walkie talkie with your stupid friends, this is ridiculous, this relationship is over!"
"This relationship is what? Over"

I went up to the missus this morning and said "I have a big problem"
She replied "Now look, you don't have a problem, we have a problem, remember our wedding day? for better for worse, for richer for poorer and all that, now what's this so called big problem"?
I said "We've got your sister pregnant"

News: Japanese princess gives up royal status to marry a commoner.
I'm certain she'll bring that up every time they have a row.

I was walking back from the pub last night when a copper pulled up in his patrol car and asked where I was going.
I said "Well, I'm actually on my way to attend a lecture on the problems of staying out late in the pub, consuming too much al-

cohol and the dangers it poses to your general health."
The copper said "Who is giving this lecture"?
I replied "My fucking missus"

I convinced the wife to work for MI5.
So she wouldn't be allowed to tell me about her day.

I bought the wife a pug dog yesterday. Despite the bulging eyes, squashed face, and rolls of fat....
The dog seems to like her.

A man goes to see a wizard and says, "Can you lift a curse that a priest put on me years ago?"
"May be" says the wizard, "Can remember the exact words of the curse?"
The man replies, "I pronounce you man and wife."

"You treat me like a dog," said my wife, "I want to sit and talk about it."
"Ok," I replied, "but not on the sofa."

Me and my mate were out having a drink when I told him that I was thinking about divorcing the missus.
He asked why and I told him that she had not spoken a word to me in over four months.
He took a long sip of his pint and said "You want to think twice before doing that, women like that are hard to find"

A bloke knocked on my door this morning and said, "Could you spare 5 minutes to do an opinion poll?"
I replied, "Sorry mate, my opinion isn't in at the moment, she's at work."

I just read a book on marriage that says treat your wife like you treated her on the first date. So after dinner tonight I'm dropping her off at her parents' house.

I accidentally handed my wife a glue stick instead of a chapstick. She still isn't talking to me.

We all have to live with the mistakes we make in life.
I have to sleep with mine as well.

Who needs a wife anyway...
How hard can it be to boil a Toast

On Saturday my pal went through the painful procedure of having his spine and both testicles removed....
Still, he got some great wedding presents though.

Most serial killers are men.
That's because women like to kill one man slowly over many many years.

My wife's just left me because I ate too much chocolate over Christmas.
I think this calls for a Celebration.

My lady isn't happy with me this frosty morning, she just told me she's going out scrape the car.
"Against what" was not the right reply

I woke up this morning and fancied a big breakfast but then I remembered my wife was sick.
She's so poorly that I had to carry her to the kitchen.

My wife recently told me: "We'd have less arguments if you weren't so pedantic". I replied, "Don't you mean 'fewer'?"

I was watching Peppa Pig this morning and my wife just walks in and turns off the Tv..
How childish is that

I was in the pub with the missus last night, and I said, "I love you."
She said, " Is that you or the beer talking?"
I replied, "It's me, talking to the beer"...

My girlfriend says she doesn't trust me.
I guess that's just one more thing she has in common with my wife.

I said to the wife "Lets go out for dinner tonight".. She replied back with that old classic "I have nothing to wear"..
so I said to her "Just put on what you wore last time we went out, you looked beautiful"..
so there we were in the local steak house, me in a t-shirt and jeans and her in her fuckin wedding dress!

I knew my marriage was in trouble that night I had a heart attack, the missus used a 2nd class stamp when she wrote for an ambulance!

I remember my wedding night, my missus got undressed and lay out spreadeagled on the bed.
She said "you know what I want don't you"?
I replied "Yes, by the looks of it, the whole fucking bed"

The police have just released my mother-in-law after questioning her about the murder of her husband.
They only spoke to her for 2 minutes before coming to the conclusion he committed suicide

Just bought the missus a nice little watch for her birthday, then realised i wasted my money.
There's a clock on the cooker.

How can you tell when your girlfriend is getting fat?
When she fits into your wife's clothes.

The wife says that I never do anything around the house, so today I planted two acorns 14ft apart in the garden.
She asked what I was doing.
I replied, starting work on my new hammock.

My wife just caught me blow drying my penis and asked what I was doing.
Apparently, "heating your dinner" was not the right answer.

My wife just walked into the living room wearing this expensive new dress she just bought on my credit card.

She said "well, what do you think?"
I said "yeah it's nice but your knickers are coming down"
She looked down and said "no their not"
I said "well the dress is going back then"

The wife said she was leaving me as I keep talking like a news reader.
More on that story later.

According Tetley tea makers, the best way to make a cuppa is to agitate the bag
So every morning I slap her lardy arse and say "Two sugars, fatty"

I bought my wife a pair of diamond earrings last month and she hasn't talked to me since. That was part of the deal.

My missus argued the other day that all I want her from is sex.
She seemed to forget all about the washing, cooking, cleaning and shopping.

I bought my missus a sexy maid's outfit in the hope that it would improve things in the bedroom.
Unfortunately it hasn't worked, the place is still a mess.

My wife was complaining that she had a head cold this morning.
I said, "Its no wonder with the amount of time it spends in the fucking fridge!".

My wife can't tell the time.
Every night I get home from the pub, she says.."what time do you call this?"

Gave the wife a handmade bra that I'd got from a craft fair, and told her it was made from sheepdog fur.
"Aww, how sweet" she giggled. "Is that to keep my boobies nice and warm?"
I said "no, but it'll round them up and point them in the right direction."

My wife has always nagged me how she would love to have a real

animal skin coat.
I've got her a beautiful donkey jacket for her birthday.

A doctor looks at recently deceased patient and asks, "What were his final words?" The nurse replies, "None, Doctor - his wife was with him to the very end."

My missus said to me "It's my birthday soon, are you going to go shopping for something that will make me look really sexy"?
I replied "OK", then went out and came back with two bottles of Jack and a crate of Stella

Since it started to rain, my wife can't stop looking through the window.
I'll have to let her in if it continues.

My wife has stood by me for 36 years.
Maybe I should let her sit down for a change.

"I wish I had a smaller bum," my wife grumbled. "Do you wish I had a smaller bum?"
"Not at all," I told her.
"Aww, you're sweet," she gushed. "Is it because you love my bum the way it is?"
"Not really," I replied. "It's because it'd look ridiculous with legs that fucking size attached to it."

I went into a shop the other day and bought some of those new super-sensitive condoms.
They're brilliant! They hang around after you fuck off and talk to the bird about "relationships"...

My missus is going through "that awkward stage" in life.
You know the one, it starts at birth and finishes on the day they fucking die.

An elderly couple had dinner at another couple's house, and after eating, the wives left the table and went into the kitchen. The two gentlemen were talking, and one said, 'Last night we went out to

a new restaurant and it was really great. . . I would recommend it very highly.'
The other man said, 'What is the name of the restaurant?'
The first man thought and thought and finally said, 'What is the name of that flower you give to someone you love? You know... The one that's red and has thorns.'
'Do you mean a rose?'
'Yes, that's the one,' replied the man.
He then turned towards the kitchen and yelled,
'Rose, what's the name of that restaurant we went to last night?

My dentist informed me today that I need a crown.
Finally, someone who understands me.

"Sarcasm will get you nowhere in life," my boss told me.
"Well, it got me to the 'International Sarcasm' finals in Santiago, Chile in 2009," I informed him.
"Really?" he asked.
"No," I replied.

In China, you get the death penalty if you don't own up to having the CoronaVirus.
It's a lose lose situation.

A farmer came upto me and said I've got 68 sheep can you round them up for me ,
I said yeah 70

I saw a poster that said, 'Have you seen my cat?'
I rang the number and told them I haven't.
I like to help where I can.

FOR ONCE AND FOR ALL MY AMERICAN FRIENDS....
It's Mum not Mom
It's crisps not chips
It's chips not fries
It's football not soccer
It's rugby not football

It's school not shooting range

A woman with a clipboard stopped me today and said, "Can I ask where you get your electricity from at the moment?"
I replied, "I'm pretty sure it comes into my house through some kind of wire."

Billy has 5 albums by Morrissey and he buys 2 more, what does Billy have?
Depression, Billy has depression.

I broke my personal record for a 100 meter sprint.
I'm now up to 57 meters.

I got sent out of class today at school for being too sarcastic.
The teacher yelled at me, "What would your parents say if I called them?' I replied, "Hello?"

To help fatties, supermarkets should help promote healthy living by putting all cakes, ice creams, pies etc. in aisles that are too narrow for the fatties to fit through.

Glasgow university evacuated as police investigate suspicious package.
Turns out it was a salad.

My boss came up to me and said "Why aren't you working?"
"I didn't see you coming." I replied.

My company does random urine tests.
To detect any traces of hope or optimism.

Twelve monks were about to be ordained. The final test was for them to line up, nude, in a garden while a nude model danced before them. Each monk had a small bell attached to his privates, and they were told that anyone whose bell rang would not be ordained because he had not reached a state of spiritual purity.
The model danced before the first monk candidate, with no reaction. She proceeded down the line with the same response until she got to the final monk. As she danced, his bell rang so loudly it

fell off and clattered to the ground. Embarrassed, he bent down to pick up the bell, and eleven other bells began to ring......

You have to question the modus operandi of people who use Latin for no reason.

I like how at the end of Hollyoaks a voice says "If you've been affected by any issues in this programme please phone this number"..
So I phoned and I said "Hello...I can't act either".

OMEGA Official Timekeeper of the Winter Olympics
TAG-HEUER Official Timekeeper of the Premier League
MICKEY MOUSE Official Timekeeper of British Rail

I am still waiting to meet a flat earth believer who has lived life on the edge.

I went for an interview for an office job today.
The interviewer told me I'd start on £2k a month and then after 6 months I'd be on £3k a month.
I told them I'd start in 6 months.

I walked out of Tesco and a guy collecting money said, "Would you like to help feed the hungry today?"
"Yes," I replied,, "That's why I've just been fucking shopping."

Jeremy Corbyn has won the respect of many pregnant women, because of his willingness to give up his seats.

Yesterday I saw a book called "How to solve 50% of your problems."
So I bought two.

In the news today, a new report says that Ryanair is the most hated airline in the country.
Ryanair has apologized to its passengers...
and charged them a £50 Apology Fee.

How many dyslexics does it take to change a lightbulb?

Steven.

Went to give a sperm sample the other day the nurse said would i like to masturbate in the cup , I said Thanks but I don't think I'm ready for a competition yet

I don't like the term 'Anal Bleaching'.
I prefer to call it 'changing my ringtone'.

If I had to describe myself in three words, I would say "Not very good at maths".

Whoever said laughter is the best medicine ...
Clearly hasn't tried curing diarrhea with a tickle fight.

I've woken up over 10,000 times and I'm still not used to it.

BREAKING: A man who took an airline to court after losing his luggage has lost his case.

This site uses cookies to ensure you get the best experience on the site. By continuing to use the site, you agree to accept these cookies.
I genuinely just copied and pasted this off the weight watchers website

I was walking in the jungle the other day when I saw a Monkey with a banana in one hand and a tin opener in the other.
I said to him "You've don't need a tin opener to peel a banana"
He replied "I know, it's for the custard"

Does anyone know how to cancel a bid on eBay?
I put one in for a Cowboy Outfit yesterday, now I'm only ten minutes away from owning Network Rail

If you think about it, we chop down bird houses to make bird houses.

I met a transvestite from the Greater Manchester area in the pub last night.
He had a Wigan address

I used to love playing knock and run when I was a kid, I still do, it's why I work for Parcel Force.

I have a chicken proof lawn.
Its impeccable.

Argos are coming to drop a wardrobe off that I bought yesterday.. I'll have to make sure that I'm home between 7.30am tomorrow and the 28th of October.

I went to a pet shop and put a sign saying 'Chameleon' next to an empty cage ......

Is it true that an apple a day keeps the doctor away?
Or is it one of Granny's myths?

I lost my job as a stage designer.
I left without making a scene.

A man with authority walks into a bar and orders everyone a round!

9 out of 10 dermatologists agree that towels are the leading cause of dry skin.

I just found out I'm colourblind. It came completely out of the Purple.

If you lose your tree, try stapling a picture of it to a cat.

My plan to steal low fat yogurt from the supermarket is taking Shape...

Without a doubt, my favourite Robin Williams movie is Mrs Fire.

Reading is just staring at a dead piece of wood and hallucinating

I met a dyslexic Yorkshire man the other day.
He was wearing a cat flap.

I was attacked by a group of mime artists.
They did unspeakable things to me.

You know what I hate? People who answer their own questions

Remember when plastic surgery was a taboo subject? Now you mention Botox and nobody raises an eyebrow.

I went into the local chemist and said to the assistant "Could I have a dozen condoms please miss"?
She said "Don't you miss me"
I said "OK, better make it thirteen then"

My girlfriend woke up with a huge smile on her face this morning. I fucking love felt tips.

They're going to put a clock on the leaning tower of Pisa. That way it'll have both the time and the inclination.

I bought the wife a hula hoop... It fits!

My mate Sid have had his ID Stolen
He's now known as S

I learn from the mistakes made by people who took my advice.

I stayed at a hotel in Blackpool recently. It overlooked the sea......unfortunately it also overlooked hygiene, good service & edible meals.

An old man drove past me on a tractor this morning and told me the end was nigh...
I think it was Farmer Gedden.

Everyone's entitled to my opinion.

Trying to understand women is like trying to smell the colour 9

Did you know that this week is National Diarrohea Week?
It runs from today until Friday

what is the difference between a hippo and a zippo? One is really heavy and the other is a little lighter.

I have just been to visit the wife's grave...

Bless her, she thinks I'm digging a pond!

If you don't believe in human perseverance you clearly haven't seen a smoker trying to use a broken lighter.

I'm not saying you should totally distrust the internet, but there's a huge discrepancy between the number of iPads I've won, and the number of iPads i own

A man in Melbourne walked into the produce section of his local supermarket and asked to buy half a head of cabbage.
The boy working in that department told him that they only sold whole heads of cabbage.
The man was insistent that the boy ask the manager about the matter.
Walking into the back room, the boy said to the manager, "Some old bastard outside wants to buy half a head of cabbage."
As he finished his sentence, he turned around to find that the man had followed and was standing right behind him, so the boy quickly added, "and this gentleman kindly offered to buy the other half."
The manager approved the deal and the man went on his way.
Later, the manager said to the boy...........
"I was impressed with the way you got yourself out of that situation earlier, we like people who can think on their feet here, where are you from son?"
"New Zealand, sir," the boy replied.
Why did you leave New Zealand ?" the manager asked.
The boy said, "Sir, there's nothing but prostitutes and rugby players there."
"Is that right?" replied the manager, "My wife is from New Zealand!"
"Really?" replied the boy, "Who did she play for?"

2000 on - ADHD.
1970 - Spoiled little bastard that needs a good slap.

Dear TAG heuer

I'm pretty sure that if I end up 500 meters under water, I won't need a fuckin' watch anymore.

My mates are really annoyed with me right now just because I lost us the pub quiz.
Apparently the drone isn't the national bird of Syria.

My mate just asked me, "If you were stuck on a desert island, and you could have 3 records, what would they be?"
I said, "The long distance swimming one would be good!"

The singer Cliff Richard has been suffering from much online abuse.
He's got himself some spying, talking, tweeting, stalking, living trolls.

Scooters...built for men who want to ride motorcycles, but prefer to feel the wind on their vaginas.

If modern society has taught us anything, it's that the less a person is qualified to have an opinion
The more likely she is to express it

If you ever feel like your life is pointless, just remember. Someone out there is fitting indicators to an Audi.

If you're going to argue publicly on a cellphone, be fair and turn the speakerphone on so everyone can hear both sides.

They say English surnames all had a meaning, as in, "Smiths" Where Blacksmiths.
"Taylors", Where Tailors
What the fuck did the Dickinsons do?

My missus is going round spreading rumours that I'm schizophrenic.
Well, three can play at that game bitch.

I saw a fortune teller the other day. She told me I would come into some money.

Last night I shagged a girl called Penny.
Wow. Spooky or what!

Why when asked "If you were to bring one item to a desert island, what would you bring?" does no one ever answer, "boat"?!

Instead of calling them flu masks, we should call them coughy filters

An old Indian Chief when asked about the practice of putting the clocks back replied....
"Only white man would think,if he cut a length off the end of his blanket and stitch it on the other end he would have a longer blanket"

My son is a man trapped in a woman's body...
He will be born in February.

Why do laxatives have a best before date?.
If they go off, what's the worst that can happen?.

How many pessimists does it take to change a lightbulb?
Why bother? The new one will just burn out too.

What is it with these Paralympians?
They can run and swim much faster than me,lift heavier weights than I can, yet they get to park much closer to Asda.

I remember the first time I ever saw an Universal Remote Control.
I thought to myself, "Well this changes everything."

University.
A place where common sense is passed off as wisdom.

I think I might have a bath.
Yep.
Just checked.
It's upstairs in the bathroom.

It isn't gender, sexuality or race that separates us
It's people who can take a joke and people who can't.

I watched a series just like the US program Breaking Bad but it was set in the UK...
It's about a guy who gets cancer and instead of starting a meth lab to pay for his treatment he goes to the NHS and its dealt with.

Doctor Who enthusiasts all over the country are up in arms about the decision to cast a female in the lead role.
They'll calm down once they get used to what a woman looks and sounds like.

My gay son called me up in tears because he wasn't allowed to join the "Social-Justice club" at his university.
I asked why they didn't let him join, and he explained that when they scanned his shoulder, they couldn't find the massive chip that should be there.

Why did the ketchup blush?
He saw the salad dressing.

Why does the mermaid wear seashells?
She outgrew her b-shells!

How is life like toilet paper?
You're either on a roll or taking shit from someone.

What does one boob say to the other boob?
If we don't get support, people will think we're nuts.

What's the difference between a G-spot and a golf ball?
A man will actually search for a golf ball.

What's a 6.9?
Another great thing screwed up by a period.

What did the banana say to the vibrator?
Why are you shaking? She's going to eat me!

What's the difference between a tire and 365 used condoms?
Ones a Goodyear. The other is a great year.

What's the difference between a pickpocket and a peeping tom? One snatches your watch. The other watches your snatch.

Did you hear about the constipated accountant? He couldn't budget, so he had to work it out with a paper and pencil.

What goes in hard and dry, but comes out soft and wet? Gum!

What's the process of applying for a job at Hooters? They just give you a bra and say, "Here, fill this out."

What's worse than waking up at a party and finding a penis drawn on your face? Finding out it was traced.

A penguin takes his car to the shop and the mechanic says it'll take about an hour for him to check it. While he waits, the penguin goes to an ice cream shop and orders a big sundae to pass the time. The penguin isn't the neatest eater, and he ends up covered in melted ice cream. When he returns to the shop, the mechanic takes one look at him and says, "Looks like you blew a seal." "No," the penguin insists, "it's just ice cream."

A family is at the dinner table. The son asks the father, "Dad, how many kinds of boobs are there?" The father, surprised, answers, "Well, son, a woman goes through three phases. In her 20s, a woman's breasts are like melons, round and firm. In her 30s and 40s, they are like pears, still nice, hanging a bit. After 50, they are like onions." "Onions?" the son asks. "Yes. You see them and they make you cry." This infuriated his wife and daughter. The daughter asks, "Mom, how many different kinds of willies are there?" The mother smiles and says, "Well, dear, a man goes through three phases also. In his 20s, his willy is like an oak tree, mighty and hard. In his 30s and 40s, it's like a birch, flexible but reliable. After his 50s, it's like a Christmas tree." "A Christmas tree?" the daughter asks. "Yes, dead from the root up and the balls are just for decoration."

A teacher is teaching a class and she sees that Johnny isn't paying attention, so she asks him, "If there are three ducks sitting on a fence, and you shoot one, how many are left?" Johnny says, "None." The teacher asks, "Why?" Johnny says, "Because the shot scared them all off." The teacher says, "No, two, but I like how you're thinking." Johnny asks the teacher, "If you see three women walking out of an ice cream parlor, one is licking her ice cream, one is sucking her ice cream, and one is biting her ice cream, which one is married?" The teacher says, "The one sucking her ice cream." Johnny says, "No, the one with the wedding ring, but I like how you're thinking!"

Why did I get divorced? Well, last week was my birthday. My wife didn't wish me a happy birthday. My parents forgot and so did my kids. I went to work and even my colleagues didn't wish me a happy birthday. As I entered my office, my secretary said, "Happy birthday, boss!" I felt so special. She asked me out for lunch. After lunch, she invited me to her apartment. We went there and she said, "Do you mind if I go into the bedroom for a minute?" "Okay," I said. She came out 5 minutes later with a birthday cake, my wife, my parents, my kids, my friends, & my colleagues all yelling, "SURPRISE!!!" while I was waiting on the sofa... naked.

After picking her son up from school one day, the mother asks him what he did at school. The kid replies, "I had sex with my teacher." She gets so mad that when they get home, she orders him to go straight to his room. When the father returns home that evening, the mother angrily tells him the news of what their son had done. As the father hears the news, a huge grin spreads across his face. He walks to his son's room and asks him what happened at school, the son tells him, "I had sex with my teacher." The father tells the boy that he is so proud of him, and he is going to reward him with the bike he has been asking for. On the way to the store, the dad asks his son if he would like to ride his new bike home. His son responds, "No thanks Dad, my butt still hurts."

A lady goes to the doctor and complains that her husband is losing interest in sex. The doctor gives her a pill, but warns her that it's still experimental. He tells her to slip it into his mashed potatoes at dinner, so that night, she does just that. About a week later, she's back at the doctor, where she says, "Doc, the pill worked great! I put it in the potatoes like you said! It wasn't five minutes later that he jumped up, raked all the food and dishes onto the floor, grabbed me, ripped all my clothes off, and ravaged me right there on the table!" The doctor says, "I'm sorry, we didn't realize the pill was that strong! The foundation will be glad to pay for any damages." "Nah," she says, "that's okay. We're never going back to that restaurant anyway."

A bride tells her husband, "Honey, you know I'm a virgin and I don't know anything about sex. Can you explain it to me first?" "Okay, sweetheart. Putting it simply, we will call your private place 'the prison' and call my private thing 'the prisoner'. So what we do is put the prisoner in the prison." And they made love for the first time and the husband was smiling with satisfaction. Nudging him, his bride giggles, "Honey the prisoner seems to have escaped." Turning on his side, he smiles and says, "Then we will have to re-imprison him." After the second time, the bride says, "Honey, the prisoner is out again!" The husband rises to the occasion and they made love again. The bride again says, "Honey, the prisoner escaped again," to which the husband yelled, "Hey, it's not a life sentence!!!"

One day, there were two boys playing by a stream. One of the young boys saw a bush and went over to it. The other boy couldn't figure out why his friend was at the bush for so long. The other boy went over to the bush and looked. The two boys were looking at a woman bathing naked in the stream. All of a sudden, the second boy took off running. The first boy couldn't understand why he ran away, so he took off after his friend. Finally, he caught up to him and asked why he ran away. The boy said to his friend, "My mom told me if I ever saw a naked lady, I would turn to stone, and I felt something getting hard, so I ran."

Two cowboys are out on the range talking about their favorite sex position. One says, "I think I enjoy the rodeo position the best." "I don't think I have ever heard of that one," says the other cowboy. "What is it?" "Well, it's where you get your girl down on all four, and you mount her from behind. Then you reach around, cup her tits, and whisper in her ear, 'boy these feel almost as nice as your sisters.' Then you try and hold on for 30 seconds."

It was Christmas Eve. A woman came home to her husband after a day of busy shopping. Later on that night when she was getting undressed for bed, he noticed a mark on the inside of her leg. "What is that?" he asked. She said, "I visited the tattoo parlor today. On the inside of one leg I had them tattoo 'Merry Christmas,' and on the inside of the other one they tattooed 'Happy New Year.'" Perplexed, he asked, "Why did you do that?" "Well," she replied, "now you can't complain that there's never anything to eat between Christmas and New Years!"

A typical macho man married a typical good looking lady, and after the wedding, he laid down the following rules. "I'll be home when I want, if I want, what time I want, and I don't expect any hassle from you. I expect a great dinner to be on the table, unless I tell you that I won't be home for dinner. I'll go hunting, fishing, boozing, and card playing when I want with my old buddies, and don't you give me a hard time about it. Those are my rules. Any comments?" His new bride said, "No, that's fine with me. Just understand that there will be sex here at seven o'clock every night, whether you're here or not."

A woman places an ad in the local newspaper. "Looking for a man with three qualifications: won't beat me up, won't run away from me, and is great in bed." Two days later her doorbell rings. "Hi, I'm Tim. I have no arms so I won't beat you, and no legs so I won't run away." "What makes you think you are great in bed?" the woman retorts. Tim replies, "I rang the doorbell, didn't I?"

A guy walks into a pub and sees a sign hanging over the bar which reads, "Cheese Sandwich: £1.50; Chicken Sandwich: £2.50; Hand

Job: £10.00." Checking his wallet for the necessary payment, he walks up to the bar and beckons to one of the three exceptionally attractive blondes serving drinks to an eager-looking group of men. "Yes?" she enquires with a knowing smile, "Can I help you?" "I was wondering," whispers the man, "Are you the one who gives the hand jobs?" "Yes," she purrs, "I am." The man replies, "Well, go wash your hands, I want a cheese sandwich!"

Three guys go to a ski lodge, and there aren't enough rooms, so they have to share a bed. In the middle of the night, the guy on the right wakes up and says, "I had this wild, vivid dream of getting a hand job!" The guy on the left wakes up, and unbelievably, he's had the same dream, too. Then the guy in the middle wakes up and says, "That's funny, I dreamed I was skiing!"

Q: Why is sex like math?
A: You add a bed, subtract the clothes, divide the legs, and pray there's no multiplying.

A trucker who has been out on the road for two months stops at a brothel outside Leeds. He walks straight up to the Madam, drops down £500 and says, "I want your ugliest woman and a grilled cheese sandwich!" The Madam is astonished. "But sir, for that kind of money you could have one of my prettiest ladies and a three-course meal." The trucker replies, "Listen darlin', I'm not horny – I'm just homesick."

A married man was having an affair with his secretary. One day, their passions overcame them in the office and they took off for her house. Exhausted from the afternoon's activities, they fell asleep and awoke at around 8 p.m. As the man threw on his clothes, he told the woman to take his shoes outside and rub them through the grass and dirt. Confused, she nonetheless complied and he slipped into his shoes and drove home. "Where have you been?" demanded his wife when he entered the house. "Darling," replied the man, "I can't lie to you. I've been having an affair with my secretary. I fell asleep in her bed and didn't wake up until eight o'clock." The wife glanced down at his shoes and said, "You liar! You've been playing golf!"

A lawyer married a woman who had previously divorced 10 husbands. On their wedding night, she told her new husband, "Please be gentle, I'm still a virgin." "What?" said the puzzled groom. "How can that be if you've been married 10 times?" "Well, Husband #1 was a sales representative. He kept telling me how great it was going to be. Husband #2 was in software services. He was never really sure how it was supposed to function, but he said he'd look into it and get back to me. Husband #3 was from field services. He said everything checked out diagnostically, but he just couldn't get the system up. Husband #4 was in telemarketing. Even though he knew he had the order, he didn't know when he would be able to deliver. Husband #5 was an engineer. He understood the basic process, but wanted three years to research, implement, and design a new state-of-the-art method. Husband #6 was from finance and administration. He thought he knew how, but he wasn't sure whether it was his job or not. Husband #7 was in marketing. Although he had a nice product, he was never sure how to position it. Husband #8 was a psychologist. All he ever did was talk about it. Husband #9 was a gynecologist. All he did was look at it. Husband #10 was a stamp collector. All he ever did was... God! I miss him! But now that I've married you, I'm really excited!" "Good," said the new husband, "but, why?" "You're a lawyer. This time I know I'm going to get screwed!"

I was sitting on my own in a restaurant, when I saw a beautiful woman at another table. I sent her a bottle of the most expensive wine on the menu. She sent me a note, "I will not touch a drop of this wine unless you can assure me that you have seven inches in your pocket." I wrote back, "Give me the wine. As gorgeous as you are, I'm not cutting off three inches for anyone."

Scientists have proven that there are two things in the air that have been known to cause women to get pregnant: their legs.

A guy and his date are parked out in the country away from town, when they start kissing and fondling each other. Just then, the girl stops and sits up. "What's the matter?" asks the guy. She replies, "I really should have mentioned this earlier, but I'm actually a prostitute, and I charge £50 for sex." The man thinks about it for a few seconds, but then reluctantly gets out a £50 note, pays her, and they have sex. After a cigarette, he just sits in the driver's seat looking out the window. "Why aren't we going anywhere?" asks the girl. "Well, I should have mentioned this before," replies the man, "but I'm actually a taxi driver, and the fare back to town is £50."

A man boards a plane with six kids. After they get settled in their seats, a woman sitting across the aisle leans over to him and asks, "Are all of those kids yours?" He replies, "No. I work for a condom company. These are customer complaints."

"Daddy, where did I come from?" seven-year-old Rachel asks. It is a moment for which her parents have carefully prepared. They take her into the living room, get out several other books, and explain all they think she should know about sexual attraction, affection, love, and reproduction. Then they both sit back and smile contentedly. "Does that answer your question?" the mom asks. "Not really," the little girl says. "Judy said she came from Oxford. I want to know where I came from."

On hearing that her elderly grandfather has just passed away, Katie goes straight to her grandparents' house to visit her 95-year-old grandmother and comfort her. When she asks how her grandfather has died, her grandmother replies, "He had a heart attack while we were making love on Sunday morning." Horrified, Katie tells her grandmother that two people nearly 100 years old having sex will surely be asking for trouble. "Oh no, my dear. Many years ago, realizing our advanced age, we figured out the best time to do it was when the church bells would start to ring. It was just the right rhythm. It was nice, slow, and even. Nothing too strenuous, simply in on the ding and out on the dong." She pauses, wipes away a tear and then continues, "And if that damned ice cream truck hadn't come along, he'd still be alive today!"

A man joins a soccer team and his new teammates inform him, "At your first team dinner as the new guy, you will have to give us a talk about sex." The evening arrives and he gives a detailed, humorous account of his sex life. When he got home, his wife asked how the evening went and not wanting to lie, but also not wanting to explain exactly what happened, he said, "Oh, I had to make a talk about yachting," his wife thought this a little peculiar but said nothing more and went to sleep. The next day she bumped into one of his new teammates at the supermarket and asked, "I heard my husband had to make a speech last night. How did it go?" His mate said smiling, 'Oh, it was excellent! Your husband is clearly very experienced!.." The wife looked confused and replied to his mate, "Strange, he has only done it twice and the second time he was sick."

Three people get arrested and are taken into holding for questioning. The officer talks to the first girl, asking, "What's your name?" She says, "Yo." The officer asks, "What are you in for?" She responds with, "Blowing bubbles." The officer takes her picture and lets her go. He asks the second girl, "What's your name?" She responds with, "Yo Yo." The officer asks, "What are you in for?" She responds with, "Blowing bubbles." The officer takes her picture and lets her go. He talks to the guy and says, "Let me guess, your name is Yo Yo Yo." The guy replies with, "No, it's Bubbles."

A wealthy man was having an affair with an Italian woman for a few years. One night, during one of their rendezvous, she confided in him that she was pregnant. Not wanting to ruin his reputation or his marriage, he paid her a large sum of money if she would go to Italy to have the child. If she stayed in Italy, he would also provide child support until the child turned 18. She agreed, but wondered how he would know when the baby was born. To keep it discrete, he told her to mail him a postcard, and write "Spaghetti" on the back. He would then arrange for child support. One day, about 9 months later, he came home to his confused wife. "Honey," she said, "you received a very strange postcard today." "Oh, just give it to me and I'll explain it later," he said. The wife handed the card over and watched as her husband read the card, turned white, and fainted. On the card was written "Spaghetti, Spaghetti, Spaghetti. Two with meatballs, one without."

One weekend, a husband is in the bathroom shaving when the local kid Bubba he hired to mow his lawn, comes in to pee. The husband slyly looks over and is shocked at how immensely endowed Bubba is. He can't help himself, and asks Bubba what his secret is. "Well," says Bubba, "every night before I climb into bed with a girl, I whack my penis on the bedpost three times. It works, and it sure impresses the girls!" The husband was excited at this easy suggestion and decided to try it that very night. So before climbing into bed with his wife, he took out his penis and whacked it three times on the bedpost. His wife, half-asleep, said, "Bubba? Is that you?"

A man saw a lady with big breasts. He asked, "Excuse me, can I bite your breasts for £1000?" She agrees, so they go to a secluded corner. She opens her blouse and the man puts his face in her breasts for 10 minutes." Eventually the lady asks, "Aren't you gonna bite them?" He replies, "No, it's too expensive."

Grandma and Grandpa were visiting their kids overnight . When Grandpa found a bottle of Viagra in his son's medicine cabinet, he asked about using one of the pills. The son said, "I don't think you should take one Dad, they're very strong and very expensive." "How much?" asked Grandpa. "£10.00 a pill," answered the son. "I don't care," said Grandpa, "I'd still like to try one, and before we leave in the morning, I'll put the money under the pillow. " Later the next morning, the son found £110 under the pillow. He called Grandpa and said, "I told you each pill was £10, not £110. "I know," said Grandpa. "The hundred is from Grandma!"

"Give it to me! Give it to me!" she yelled, "I'm so wet, give it to me now!" She could scream all she wanted to. I was keeping the umbrella.

A nun and a priest were crossing the Sahara desert on a camel. On the third day out the camel suddenly dropped dead without warning. After dusting themselves off, the nun and the priest surveyed their situation. After a long period of silence, the priest spoke. "Well sister, this looks pretty grim." "I know, father." "In fact, I don't think it likely that we can survive more than a day or two." "I agree." "Sister, since we are unlikely to make it out of here alive, would you do something for me?" "Anything father." "I have never seen a woman's breasts and I was wondering if I might see yours." "Well, under the circumstances I don't see that it would do any harm." The nun opened her habit and the priest enjoyed the sight of her shapely breasts, commenting frequently on their beauty. "Sister would you mind if I touched them?" She consented and he fondled them for several minutes. "Father, could I ask something of you?" "Yes sister?" "I have never seen a man's penis. Could I see yours?" "I supposed that would be OK," the priest replied lifting his robe. "Oh father, may I touch it?" This time the priest consented and after a few minutes of fondling he was sporting a huge erection. "Sister, you know that if I insert my penis in the right place, it can give life." "Is that true father?" "Yes it is, sister." "Then why don't you stick it up that camel's ass and lets get the hell out of here."

A boy walks in on his mom and dad having sex. He asks, "What are you doing?" The dad replies, "Making you a brother or sister!" The boy says, "Well, do her doggy style I want a puppy."

An old man goes to a church, and is making a confession:
Man: "Father, I am 75 years old. I have been married for 50 years. All these years I had been faithful to my wife, but yesterday I was intimate with an 18 year old."
Father: "When was the last time you made a confession?"

Man: "I never have, I am Jewish."
Father: "Then why are telling me all this?"
Man: "I'm telling everybody!"

Two men visit a prostitute. The first man goes into the bedroom. He comes out ten minutes later and says, "Heck. My wife is better than that." The second man goes in. He comes out ten minutes later and says, "You know? Your wife IS better."

A man and his wife go to their honeymoon hotel for their 25th anniversary. As the couple reflected on that magical evening 25 years ago, the wife asked the husband, "When you first saw my naked body in front of you, what was going through your mind?" The husband replied, "All I wanted to do was to fuck your brains out, and suck your tits dry." Then, as the wife undressed, she asked, "What are you thinking now?" He replied, "It looks as if I did a pretty good job."

There was an elderly man who wanted to make his younger wife pregnant. He went to the doctor to get a sperm count. The doctor told him to take a specimen cup home, fill it, and bring it back. The elderly man came back the next day; the specimen cup was empty and the lid was on it. The doctor asked, "What was the problem?" The elderly man said, "Well, I tried with my right hand... nothing. I tried with my left hand... nothing. So my wife tried with her right hand... nothing. Her left hand... nothing. Her mouth... nothing. Then my wife's friend tried. Right hand, left hand, mouth... still nothing. The doctor replied, "Wait a minute, did you say your wife's friend too?!" The elderly man answered, "Yeah, and we still couldn't get the lid off of the specimen cup."

A man is walking down the street, when he notices that his grandfather is sitting on the porch in a rocking chair, with nothing on from the waist down. "Grandpa, what are you doing?" the man exclaims. The old man looks off in the distance and does not answer his grandson. "Grandpa, what are you doing sitting out here with nothing on below the waist?" he asks again. The old man slyly looks at him and says, "Well, last week I sat out here with no shirt on, and I got a stiff neck. This was your Grandma's idea!"

There is more money being spent on breast implants and Viagra today, than on Alzheimer's research. This means that by 2040, there should be a large elderly population with perky boobs, huge erections, and absolutely no recollection of what to do with them.

A professor was giving a lecture on involuntary muscular contractions to his first year medical students. Realizing that this was not the most riveting subject, he decided to lighten the mood. He pointed to a young woman in the front row and asked, "Do you know what your asshole is doing while you're having an orgasm?" She replied, "He's probably playing golf with his friends."

Interviewer: "What's your greatest weakness?"
Candidate: "Honesty."
Interviewer: "I don't think honesty is a weakness."
Candidate: "I don't give a fuck what you think."

A child asked his father, "How were people born?" So his father said, "Adam and Eve made babies, then their babies became adults and made babies, and so on." The child then went to his mother, asked her the same question and she told him, "We were monkeys then we evolved to become like we are now." The child ran back to his father and said, "You lied to me!" His father replied, "No, your mom was talking about her side of the family."

Q: Is Google male or female?
A: Female, because it doesn't let you finish a sentence before making a suggestion.

Girlfriend: "Am I pretty or ugly?"
Boyfriend: "You're both."
Girlfriend: "What do you mean?"
Boyfriend: "You're pretty ugly."

Bob was in trouble. He forgot his wedding anniversary. His wife was really angry. She told him "Tomorrow morning, I expect to find a gift in the driveway that goes from 0 to 200 in 6 seconds AND IT BETTER BE THERE!" The next morning he got up early and left for work. When his wife woke up, she looked out the window and sure enough there was a box gift-wrapped in the middle of the driveway. Confused, the wife put on her robe and ran out to the driveway, brought the box back in the house. She opened it and found a brand new bathroom scale. Bob has been missing since Friday.

Ralph is driving home one evening, when he suddenly realizes that it's his daughter's birthday and he hasn't bought her a present. He drives to the mall, runs to the toy store, and says to the shop assistant, "How much is that Barbie in the window?" In a condescending manner, she says, "Which Barbie?" She continues, "We have Barbie Goes to the Gym for £19.95, Barbie Goes to the Ball for £19.95, Barbie Goes Shopping for £19.95, Barbie Goes to the Beach for £19.95, Barbie Goes Nightclubbing for £19.95, and Divorced Barbie for £265.00." Ralph asks, "Why is the Divorced Barbie £265.00 when all the others are only £19.95?" "That's obvious," the saleslady says. "Divorced Barbie comes with Ken's house, Ken's car, Ken's boat, Ken's furniture..."

A police officer attempts to stop a car for speeding and the guy gradually increases his speed until he's topping 100 mph. The man eventually realizes he can't escape and finally pulls over. The cop approaches the car and says, "It's been a long day and my shift is almost over, so if you can give me a good excuse for your behavior, I'll let you go." The guy thinks for a few seconds and then says, "My wife ran away with a cop about a week ago. I thought you might be that officer trying to give her back!"

After Brian proposed to Jill, his father took him to one side. "Son, when I first got married to your mother, the first thing I did when we got home was take off my pants. I gave them to your mother and told her to try them on, which she did. They were huge on her and she said that she couldn't wear them because they were too large. I said to her, 'Of course they are too big for you, I wear the pants in this family and I always will.' Ever since that day, son, we have never had a single problem." Brian took his dad's advice and did the same thing to his wife on his wedding night. Then, Jill took off her panties and gave them to Brian. "Try these on," she said. Brian went along with it and tried them on, but they were far too small. "What's the point of this? I can't get into your panties," said Brian. "Exactly," Jill replied, "and if you don't change your attitude, you never will!"

A man escapes from prison where he has been for 15 years. He breaks into a house to look for money and guns, and finds a young couple in bed. He orders the guy out of bed and ties him to a chair. He ties the girl to the bed and he gets on top of her, kisses her neck, and then gets up and goes into the bathroom. While he's in there, the husband tells his wife, "Listen, this guy is an escaped convict, look at his clothes! He probably spent lots of time in jail and hasn't seen a woman in years. I saw how he kissed your neck. If he wants sex, don't resist, don't complain, do whatever he tells you. Satisfy him no matter how much he nauseates you. This guy is probably very dangerous. If he gets angry, he'll kill us. Be strong, honey. I love you." His wife responds, "He wasn't kissing my neck. He was whispering in my ear. He told me he was gay, thought you were cute, and asked me if we had any Vaseline. I told him it was in the bathroom. Be strong honey. I love you, too!"

A man asks his wife, "What would you do if I won the lottery?" His wife says, "Take half and leave your ass!" The man replies, "Great! I won £10, here is a fiver, now get out!"

Reaching the end of a job interview, the Human Resources Officer asks a young engineer fresh out of Cambridge, "And what starting salary are you looking for?" The engineer replies, "In the region of £125,000 a year, depending on the benefits package." The interviewer inquires, "Well, what would you say to a package of five weeks vacation, 14 paid holidays, full medical and dental, company matching retirement fund to 50% of salary, and a company car leased every two years, say, a red Corvette?" The engineer sits up straight and says, "Wow! Are you kidding?" The interviewer replies, "Yeah, but you started it."

Q: Why did the can crusher quit his job?
A: Because it was soda pressing.

How is Christmas like your job? You do all the work and the fat guy in the suit gets all the credit.

An government organization is like a tree full of monkeys, all on different limbs at different levels. The monkeys on top look down and see a tree full of smiling faces. The monkeys on the bottom look up and see nothing but assholes.

A lawyer runs a stop sign and gets pulled over by a sheriff. He thinks he's smarter being a big shot lawyer from New York and has a better education than an sheriff from West Virginia. The sheriff asks for license and registration. The lawyer asks, "What for?" The sheriff responds, "You didn't come to a complete stop at the stop sign." The lawyer says, "I slowed down and no one was coming." "You still didn't come to a complete stop. License and registration please," say the sheriff impatiently. The lawyer says, "If you can show me the legal difference between slow down and stop, I'll give you my license and registration and you can give me the ticket. If not, you let me go and don't give me the ticket." The sheriff says, "That sounds fair, please exit your vehicle." The lawyer steps out and the sheriff takes out his nightstick and starts beating the lawyer with it. The sheriff says, "Do you want me to stop or just slow down?"

Two factory workers are talking. The woman says, "I can make the boss give me the day off." The man replies, "And how would you do that?" The woman says, "Just wait and see." She then hangs upside down from the ceiling. The boss comes in and says, "What are you doing?" The woman replies, "I'm a light bulb." The boss then says, "You've been working so much that you've gone crazy. I think you need to take the day off." The man starts to follow her and the boss says, "Where are you going?" The man says, "I'm going home, too. I can't work in the dark."

A boss said to his secretary, "I want to have sex with you, but I will make it very fast. I'll throw £1,000 on the floor and by the time you bend down to pick it up, I'll be done." She thought for a moment then called her boyfriend and told him the story. Her boyfriend said, "Do it but ask him for £2,000. Then pick up the money so fast, he won't even have enough time to undress himself." She agrees. After half an hour passes, the boyfriend calls the girlfriend and asks, "So what happened?" She responds, "The bastard used coins, so I'm still picking it up and he is still having sex with me!"

Teacher: "Kids, what does the chicken give you?"
Student: "Meat!"
Teacher: "Very good! Now what does the pig give you?"
Student: "Bacon!"
Teacher: "Great! And what does the fat cow give you?"
Student: "Homework!"

My friend thinks he is smart. He told me an onion is the only food that makes you cry, so I threw a coconut at his face.

Kid 1: "Hey, I bet you're still a virgin."
Kid 2: "Yeah, I was a virgin until last night ."
Kid 1: "As if."
Kid 2: "Yeah, just ask your sister."
Kid 1: "I don't have a sister."
Kid 2: "You will in about nine months."

A teacher wanted to teach her students about self-esteem, so she asked anyone who thought they were stupid to stand up. One kid stood up and the teacher was surprised. She didn't think anyone would stand up so she asked him, "Why did you stand up?" He answered, "I didn't want to leave you standing up by yourself."

Whenever your ex says, "You'll never find someone like me," the answer to that is, "That's the point."

Light travels faster than sound. This is why some people appear bright until you hear them speak.

BOOKS BY THIS AUTHOR

Jokes To Keep You Occupied During Isolation

Jokes to keep you amused during the worldwide Lockdown of 2020.
All profits got towards care workers who have put themselves on the front line to look after the elderly

Printed in Great Britain
by Amazon